Riverbank Memories
By Mike Watts

Dedicated to my family
Phyllis, Christie, Rivers, and Drew

"Thank you for your inspiration, love, and support."

A special thanks also to my lifelong fishing buddies: Dave and Meta Armstrong, Mike Harvell, George Campbell, Jimmy Davis, Sally Armstrong, and Mike Bridges.

Thanks also to Larry Chesney, editor of *riversandfeathers.com*, for guidance and support. Other mentors along the journey include Jim Mize, Michael Altizer, and Joey Frazier.

Prepared For Publishing by **Book Publishing Pulse** (https://bookpublishingpulse.com/)

First edition [2024]

Table of Contents

Introduction

From the Author

Riverbank Memories is a covey of short stories, recollections, and past memories encompassing fly fishing, a few adventures, and the family. After chasing trout with a fly rod in the Southern Appalachians and beyond for more than four decades, it was time to assemble these thoughts and notes in one place.

Writing this book was a journey. After many years of support and coaxing from Phyllis and Christie, I cataloged a few stories under one cover. Throughout the book, you will find some nontruths, tall tales, all half-remembered stories that were originally scribbled in a pile of notes stuck inside folders. Many of the following stories were taken from journals, written on 3x5 index cards, and a faded composition book written in the late 1970s, '80s, and forward. My faded and penciled hieroglyphic handwriting composed notes with incomplete sentences and no punctuation, making deciphering them difficult decades later. Honestly, my cursive handwriting has been referred to as a collection of wavy lines with intervals of wasted ink thrown in for confusion. The fun in rewriting some of the stories was the trip they led me down memory lane.

Wading mountain streams, hiking to new waters, and looking for new places to cast a fly offer some respite from modern-day society. The sport has played a vital role in helping me to keep a sense of sanity and clarity over the years. It's not always about the fish, but catching one helps. There have been days when I was excited to at least hook one. As my long-time fishing buddy, Mike Harvell, once said, "I don't mind sometimes not catching fish; I just hate it when I have to work real hard at it."

Most of the stories have fly fishing overtones. I couldn't help it. It's my passion, and I like to share. But this is not totally a fly fishing book.

As you read, you will find scattered short stories about kids playing outdoors and being mischievous. For some reason, these stories came naturally. No outdoor book is complete without a few dog stories. I was fortunate to have Kasper, a black Labrador for twelve years. She was a great dog, willing to retrieve whatever I was lucky enough to hit, but she was a family dog first.

I've been blessed to have fished and hunted with great people in many respects. Their attributes are defined by their unshakeable friendship, deep conviction for conservation, willingness to share their personal affection for nature, and propensity to handle an enormous amount of trash-talking.

I affectionately call these folks my "fishing family." We've been on adventures chasing fish from West to East, and North to South, always searching to see what's around the next bend or hiding below a dock. There have been decades of laughs, fishing tales, jokes, pranks, lies, and flies. We never left home without bail money and a lawyer's mobile phone number.

Composing a book is a lot of work. Without the patience of my wife, Phyllis, this book would have never become a reality. She has "put up with a lot" as I rambled in search of game and fish and never complained. She affectionately called me "nuts" or "crazy." Her friendly smile upon my return still warms my heart even though I may be tired, dirty, ornery, wet, sometimes cold, and may have tracked mud into the house.

She questioned my judgment when I would purchase new waders and camouflage clothing instead of dress shoes and shirts for work. In my opinion, flip-flops match any outfit. On one occasion, I couldn't determine whether she was embarrassed, mad, or laughing when I told the preacher that I wouldn't see him on Sundays until after deer season. However, I promised to sit in a tree, still hunting, and pray for him.

I hope this entertaining publication will make you smile and reminisce about someplace you might have been.

Home Waters

"Poets talk about 'spots of time,' but it is really fishermen who experience eternity compressed into a moment. No one can tell what a spot is until suddenly the whole world is a fish and the fish is gone."
~Norman MacLean, "A River Runs Through It."

Home Water

I have never figured out why a clear, cold-running river can captivate me to return again and again to the same particular stretch of water. If you fish for any length of time, there will be a defining moment when that special place appears, and you will know it. I have my special place. It's not a secret place, but a person has to look hard to find it. I call it my home water.

It's a 30-minute stroll down through the woods on an unkempt and somewhat overgrown path. Ambling along the path, I step into a cathedral of an old, north-facing mountain-growth forest where the damp, moist smell permeates. I try to imagine how it looked 100 years ago before forestation. Was this path here? Who used it?

Sometimes, I'm asked how I regularly navigate back to exactly the same spot.

It's easy. Little reminders resonate in my memory as I walk. I have only to remember the starting point, and everything else seems to fall in place.

Even though the forest manifests itself differently with every passing season, the path remains constant. I found this path by accident four decades ago. I had pulled off the road to the park, aiming to walk to another section of the river, when I spied a little path leading off in a different direction up the mountain. I thought maybe this old, worn stretch of dirt might indeed be 'the road less traveled', and it prompted an investigation. One that I have since been grateful for taking.

The trail was somewhat overgrown and lay partially hidden, inviting my curiosity to follow. It began with a quick ascent up the mountain, meandering along several switchbacks. Then it gently flowed downhill into a valley.

As I approach the valley, a lower beech limb has gotten tip-heavy with growth and created an arbor over the path, like a sign blinking "Enter Here." Once inside the arbor, the path turns slightly downhill again. It is here that ferns grow undisturbed. In late spring and summer, they are silvery gray, green and very thick. Their leaves catch the indirect sun that has broken through the canopy and ignite this valley with a blanket of iridescent light green. Interspersed with the smaller ferns are the larger cinnamon ferns, which transcend above them. I always stop and gaze in awe.

After a short hike, I begin to hear the river, its various melodic pitches as water splashes over rocks, making music with its ever-creating current and flows.

As I approach the river and listen, the runs, riffles, and bubbly foam lines speak their language as if to say "hello." That old sycamore stump hasn't rotted out yet. Towering only about 15 feet now, I can remember its silhouette against the mountain background. This mighty protector of the stream bank was pierced with lightning one summer evening and slowly died in winter, its leaves never to shade that section again. The river flows constantly change, and so does everything connected.

Underneath its branches there is a deep crevice in the river bottom that consistently held fish until the tree fell. Now, only a graveside stump remains as a tombstone to mark its existence. Days of dropping inchworm patterns and floating hoppers over the pool don't yield the fish once caught there. But I still fish it anyway, for memories.

It was a tight cast to land the fly underneath the lowest limb above the water line. Proper positioning was the key prior to flipping a roll cast accurately. Many hours of fly tying remained hung on its secondary branches, only to rust and dissolve in the weather. The river's moodiness is more chronic now with the shade gone, but it continues to flow cold and clear.

Time and life sometimes create a separation of visits, but walking back into that familiar place and hearing the water cascading over rocks, I acknowledge that "it's good to be back home." I quietly whisper this soliloquy every time.

Stream banks flourish, and parts erode over time; sandbars wash and rocks move during high water and excessive rainfall. Currents alter the river's course and navigate through this maze to move, deepen, and shallow out pools and eddies. This can make wading a challenge. Weather and time convert the once linear foam lines into a puzzle of cross currents that zig-zag downstream. Sometimes temporary until the next storm, its complexion may change, but its moodiness prevails. This is my home water.

Sometimes, I have gone years before returning. But I continue to think of the good times I've had there: the fish, the companionship, and the solitude. Am I haunted by the river, or is there some magnetic, interpersonal attraction it has with me? Is it because I have become familiar with it over time and feel comfortable strapping on wading boots and feeling its currents?

It may be the same stretch of river day after day, year after year, but within each day, it develops a unique and temporary persona. The same fly, fished at the same time, in the same run but a different day, and no takers.
"What happened?"
"What changed?"
"Where did the fish go?"
Perplexed and frustrated with a hint of anxiety, I merely fish on, understanding that home waters giveth and taketh away, and be honored to be there when it giveth! I always come back either way.

This is not just one person's river, never to be shared. It's there for everyone to feel its mood and be challenged to immerse themselves in this watery bit of heaven. There are miles of river to fish, but the heart and river knowledge, coupled with a hint of confidence, keep this particular stretch special. It's known to me as my home water.

Happy Place

Does everyone have a happy place? This could be defined as a place in one's mind where one displaces their present location, escapes their present circumstances, totally ignores current events around them, and smiles with a sense of warmth and assurance wherever this happy place" might be. And outwardly smile while you are thinking about it.

What ignites a person to get to their happy place quickly? Is it sitting on the porch reminiscing with friends over a beverage? In a cubicle at work, trying to de-stress from office commotion? Or the ubiquitous conference call, or should we refer to it now as a Zoom call, where you mute the microphone and turn off the camera? Then you sit there and stare at unseen words, wishing you were someplace else? You hear your name mentioned and embarrassingly ask for the question to be repeated when the conversation was only referring to you and not asking you anything.

Can you find that happy place taking your wife to Talbots and sitting in the "King" chair in the middle of the showroom, telling strangers how nice they look in those fashionable clothes as they parade throughout the store, grabbing handfuls of apparel to take back to the dressing room? Or better yet, take a trip to the happy place while committed to watching Lifetime movies on a Sunday night instead of *North Woods Law*.

How does one define a happy place? Does it hinge with a hint of frustration such as thinking about the large buck I saw last season while climbing a tree stand? My rifle was tied to a rope and laying unloaded on the ground as the buck walked by just a few yards away from where I knew he would. Or the turkey that gobbled for two hours only to finally attract five females within hearing distance? His harem was in order, and he didn't need some stubborn, yelping hen that couldn't take orders and come to him. He took the easy ones and walked off to breed.

Why didn't I strip set the hook on that redfish instead of merely lifting the rod up like I have done for 45 years on trout? I knew better and had gone over and over that hook-setting response in my head on the three-hour ride to Charleston. To make matters worse, it was a nice fish and the video in my mind of it swimming off will never leave me. Then there was the tongue thrashing I received from my buddy poling the flats boat, skimming silently across the salt marsh. I listened to a descriptive detail again on how to strip set the hook set. I could only look sheepish and offer an understanding nod.

The deal with the happy place is when I'm there, I never get tired or feel pain. The river is always at the perfect height, and the fish are always rising. I have only one fly, and the fish take it readily.

The bass are in the same pre-spawn, hungry mood as the last time I visited. The lake is clear, and the fish are on the same point as last year.

I can remember there were no beads of sweat on the long, predawn walk to the deer stand in early September. The little chickadees and sparrows had not awakened to startle or flutter to give away my location as I approached my destination. The moon was full, and I didn't need a flashlight. My steps were silent along the path, and was careful not to warn Split Toe I was nearby.

I remember one January on the river. The mountain river is edged with ice diamonds bordering the shoals. The mist where water bounced off rocks has frozen where it splashed. These iced diamonds twinkle with sunlight, giving the river an expensive look. My waders freeze when not submerged and the ice in my rod guides make it tough to cast. But standing here looking downstream at the river bordered by mountain tops in winter makes me happy. I am not cold.

There were December mornings when incessant flocks of ducks circled and would cup their wings on point and aim at a hole in my decoys with just a few feeding chuckles. There are no hail calls or pleading, just willing mallards coming in to meet new friends.

It doesn't matter how severe the weather is; it is totally irrelevant in my happy place. The rice fields here in Arkansas are half frozen over, and the ice line is growing. The temperature is in the single digits, but I am warm. I can still feel all my fingers and don't even think about the hand warmers I brought. Gloves are sufficient. Moisture from my nose has frozen my mustache and the hairs are stiff. They may turn brittle and fall out, but I don't care. They'll grow back. The sunrise brings with it a vision of ducks from all directions. It's not cold because I am happy.

Spring dogwood blooms signal the March Brown mayfly hatch has begun on the Chattooga River. In my mind, I purposely drive by several pastures to make sure the cows are feeding. Dogwoods are blooming in the background, and cattle feeding signals there are feeding fish, so I turn off the next interstate exit and head north. Maybe no one will call as the phone service is suspect. I don't really care as I am headed to my happy place.

Despite all the happy places we think about, there is still that one special place that not only brings a smile but makes my heart warm and last several lifetimes. Mine is sharing the outdoors with my grandson, Rivers, watching him experience all that we take for granted for the first time. Looking at the world from a forgotten perspective makes me young again. Everything old to me is new to him.

"Let's tie 'fishes', Papa!" he says with an innocent, learning voice. All the fly-tying materials, paints, and tools intrigue him. "Cut the hook off, Papa, so we don't hurt the fish," he says. "I don't use hooks either, son. They just love my 'fishes' so much that they swallow them whole, and I release them," I reply.

His first fish was a catfish. As I hold him back on the dock, I can feel his excitement as he grits his teeth and grinds the spinning reel gears with all his strength until the fish finally yields.

The beach is a sandy wonderland. I run after him as he is screaming, excitedly waving his hands, and chasing seagulls and sandpipers. And then the boat ride. He must drive. Every toggle switch is flipped on, and he throws the throttle forward as the bow rises. He squeezes my arm and laughs.

However, there is always a reality check when we visit our happy place. The phone does ring: another business call. I pull the truck over to the side of the road, answer the phone, and check emails. My happy place has disappeared, instantaneously gone. Temporarily cataloged and filed away in the Dewey Decimal System of my mind. I'll be back one day soon and hope to find more happy places.

My River

Spring bleeds into summer, sometimes impatiently, as the days continue to lengthen. Along with the heat and humidity, we temporarily lose the solitude the river provides this time of year and must share it with others. Kayakers, inner tubers, and swimmers have their place on the river, too.

Usually, by early evening, the river gets some needed respite from the summer traffic and offers a chance for me to squeeze in my own time there. Even the local wildlife understands the solace the approaching sunset provides. On this particular evening, a brief thunderstorm has scattered the visitors, and I'm alone, except for the wildlife that calls this place home.

On every river, there is a special place where nature kindly lends us a few fish on every outing. Maybe because we know it intimately, or maybe it's just plain luck. Out of respect, I never abuse the rivers' generosity but nurture this special fish-giving place with reverence. On this evening, I quietly slip through the woods with no real path to follow, just local knowledge, and ease down the riverbank to my secret access point.

Once there, I stand on the riverbank, listening and observing. It's been a year since I have been back to my favorite spot. I've thought of it often but couldn't make the journey. As I near the river, I can hear the water cascading over rocks and emptying into plunge pools, scenes I've relived on many occasions.

There is something special in the river's solitude at dusk. Standing along the river edge in knee-deep, cold, flowing water, my sense of awareness begins to dominate. I look for little things that repetition and experience taught me. I have decided to wet wade instead of donning waders, hoping to put me in closer touch with the river I love. I've been here before, hundreds of times over the years. This place is just a fishing magnet that keeps pulling me back.

My resting rock never moves. Sticking just high enough out of the water, I can stand and lean back against it and remain hidden and motionless, but I am still able to roll cast. Despite the monsoons, floods, and heavy rains that have changed the river bottom, creating new pools and riffles, this rock remains steadfast. It's hard to ponder this river section without thinking about this rock. I occasionally look over my shoulder to make sure a creature with no legs isn't trying to share my rock space, or is it sharing its' space with me?

Looking up between the treetops, I notice stoneflies flittering against the gray sky. A good indication of water quality. The shrill call from a startled pair of wood ducks swimming in the eddy behind me breaks the moment. I must have spooked them as I eased around my rock and they saw me intruding.

Caddisflies, with their tent-shaped wings, skitter against the foam line along a river seam of polished rocks, leaving a wake as they dry their wings before flight. It's a concert dance, specially choreographed for me. I never get tired or bored watching a river reveal its community. And not a single fish is feeding on them.

I'm also happy to see my favorite little yellow mayfly. During this time of year, mayflies have never disappointed, emerging from their nymphal shucks on the river bottom and swimming to the surface to display their soft yellow outfits.

Trout like to greet them also. But the mayflies' abundance has always outweighed the meals they provide the fish. With darkness approaching, I decided to fish only dry flies on the surface. With the fading light also goes my fading eyesight. After I tie on a fly, I test the knot for strength. Later, the fading light will prevent me from threading another hook eye should I break off or get tangled.

A deep pool against the far bank was always the gathering point of several nice runs. The river seemed to channel itself into this pool, and it was there my success reigned during years gone by. My rock was the perfect observation point. Despite the forces of nature, my little section of the river withstood the beating.

A small splash fades quickly in the head of the run, and had I not been looking in that direction, I would have probably missed it. It's a good sign of things to come. Another rise below the first one. An eruption in the pool where the current begins to slow. A dainty little mayfly survives and flutters up and off. And so it begins.

I hadn't cast yet, still absorbing the river in its majestic entirety. I just continue to watch and make memories. Several more fish rise, but nothing like the earlier explosion. As the insect hatch continues with more frequency, wily trout begin looking up and enjoying the meal the river provides.

I roll cast across, throw an upriver mend, and my fly floats delicately among the naturals. A splash and I lift the rod tip up and a nice, wild brown dives and thrashes among the connecting currents. The old cane rod feels perfect in hand. Its sensitivity vibrates the rod tip halfway down as the fish turns, twists, and pulls against the current. The English-made Hardy Princess reel drag clicks loudly a few notes, and I succumb to this nostalgic moment. The beautiful brown is brought to hand and gently released.

It's almost dark now, and I decide to lean back again on "my rock," inhale and hold my breath, hoping to stop time for a few brief moments. It doesn't work, but I have this all pictured in my mind to file and bring up another day.

In the dark, wading down the river is tricky, so I stay close to the edge. It's a hundred yards to the fallen hemlock facing downriver underneath an old stump, which props the tree up just high enough to allow me to crawl under. I find my path. It's easy to follow.

The flashlight should probably be turned on as I meander back to the truck, but then again, it would take away from the light show. Like a magic wand waving brilliant yellow sparkles, thousands of fireflies illuminate the woods, lighting the way. It's a wonderful ending to a great date with the river. I consider myself lucky to have been a participant with a front-row seat in this outdoor theater.

The Complicated Art of Pond Fishing

How did life get so complicated? How does one make the left turn to an exaggerated state of busyness? I have handwritten notes to remind me where the other handwritten notes are located so I won't forget what the fourth note said if I can find where I put it! Seems as if the wheels of my thought process move faster than the rest of me can catch up with at times. Of course, it bleeds over into my fishing.

I had the opportunity to spend an entire weekend fishing ponds located in different geographical areas of the state of South Carolina. I had never seen, much less fished them, and many decisions seemed to complicate my entire pre-fishing ritual.

Going to a new area rendered decision-making difficult. One pond was located near the southwest border of South Carolina, while the second pond was located near the center of the state. Unknown answers to my questions would only be revealed when I visibly laid eyes on these bodies of water. But I did need to prepare for the expedition at hand. Meanwhile, I would struggle with the ailment known as "tackleholicism." This affliction usually rears its ugly head whenever I venture off to a new "unknown" place to fish.

"How much stuff do I really need to carry? What were the ponds like, heavy with lily pads stretching out to a swamp? Do I take the seven-weight fly rod, or are the six- and maybe the five-weight rods sufficient? Should I grab the stiff saltwater rods for the wind? Or do I just grab all rods of various sizes to be ready to handle all situations?"

Now, I must think about reels and lines. If I throw topwater, then a floating line is in order, but which size rod would I use? Lily pads need heavier lines to pull the fish out. If I decide to throw streamers, a medium sink tip to get the fly down a little deeper is required. Should I just bring the top water assortment of flies or include the streamer box and nymph assortment? And not to forget my flybox(es); is there anything I need to tie before I leave? Why do I always over-tie the number of flies for a trip only to find out I didn't have the right ones anyway?

Fly type and size would also determine what size tippet I need to preassemble my leaders. Also, thoughts about the pond types crossed my mind. Are they tannic stained from organic matter or spring-fed and crystal clear as drinking water in a glass? If they are overgrown with grass and lily pads, do I need to bring my weedless fly selection?

Would there be a small boat to use at either pond? Is the battery charged for the trolling motor, or would I have to paddle? Should I worry about bringing a marine trolling motor battery? Or do I need to bring boots to wade the pond's edge and be on snake and alligator alert?

As packing and gathering began, the mancave looked like a fly shop on Black Friday! Miscellaneous equipment, fly rods from different manufacturers, multiple fly boxes, rain gear, and a kayak paddle were laid neatly on the floor. It looked organized to me, though my wife thought differently. Unsure of conditions, the element of surprise, and coupled with pre-fishing excitement, it was finally decision time. What to pack?

Decisions were finally made and the truck loaded. In three hours I would stand in a new frontier to sore lip some fish. My preparations were replayed a thousand times over in my mind the entire trip. I hope there is never a time when I quit being excited about a fishing trip and the actual act of fishing.

On this trip, the Jon boats I used on both ponds took on water, one more than the other. On the first pond, I realized it was time to get back to land when the duck decoy lying in the back stern floor almost floated out. Luckily, the trolling motor battery had enough juice to get me back.

At the second pond, I took a 12-ounce Solo cup and used it to constantly bale the incoming water in order to provide a few good hours of fishing. Fish were caught, and memories were made. And the one fly rod I grabbed along with a handful of flies provided a "simpleton "many hours of enjoyment!

Dreams and Desires

One great thing about fly fishing is that after a while, nothing exists of the world but thoughts of fly fishing." ~ Norman Maclean

A Great Day After All

"One great thing about fly fishing is that after a while, nothing exists of the world but thoughts of fly fishing." Norman Maclean

Suppose you're somewhat of a fly fishing 'newbie', excited about this new sport but inexperienced, and you find yourself standing among three seasoned fly fishermen.

Intimidating? Definitely. But you listen intensely, trying to absorb every tidbit of information, even if the conversation sounds like a foreign language. Grandpa used to call that "stealing with your ears!"

Newbie had been wading the river and flailing casts all morning with no luck. He had seen several fish rise, dimpling and feeding on the surface. Newbie tried to entice them with a dry fly, but no luck.

Later, he switched to nymphs and used split shots with multiple flies trying to pick up a fish deep. He had only been fly fishing for a few months and was excited about this new passion, one that he hoped would last a lifetime. At this rate, he thought it would take a lifetime to learn. But he was determined to crack the code to success. Newbie was totally hooked on fly fishing. If only he could hook one fish on a fly that day. Surely, he had a fly that would make a trout bite.

Tired, discouraged, and needing to take a break, he waded around a sharp turn in the river. As he walked upstream around the bend, he noticed three fishermen resting against a mossy boulder, chatting nonchalantly. They looked to be experienced, judging from their attire, and he thought he could probe them for some fish-catching tips.

As he neared the group gathered by the water's edge, he noticed several flasks of spirits being passed around. Each fisherman would take a sip, then interrupt the others, bragging about a particular fish that had succumbed to their fly. They were oblivious to Newbie's approach.

He thought this small group of veteran fly fishermen reeked of knowledge that should be probed. The two oldest fellows had long grayish-white hair which protruded from dirty, sweaty long-billed hats, one tipped back on a forehead and one hat cocked sideways. Newbie surmised their sunburnt, aged, unshaven faces showed wisdom, experience, and long days spent wading rivers.

As he walked closer to them, he became more intrigued when he peered closely at their fly rods, all gently sandwiched into small limbs of a laurel bush nearby to prevent them from falling over and being stepped on. He noticed one was an old bamboo two-piece rod with a Hardy Princess reel. The second one appeared to be a brown fiberglass rod with an Orvis Madison reel. The third was extremely long, probably 10 feet, made of graphite or boron with a small reel filled with brightly colored lines.

Their conversation seemed intense, but Newbie decided this was a perfect time to gain local knowledge.

"Hey guys, how is the fishing today?" he asked. Noticing a gap in their circle, he eased into the opening, hoping to soak up information and a sip of whatever was in the flask.

"Pretty good," said one of the older, more crusty-looking fellows.

Realizing his entry into the conversation had caused an awkward silence, Newbie quickly fired off another question.

"Whatcha catch 'em on?" he inquired hopefully.

The youngest in the group, a 70ish fellow affectionately referred to as the Kid by the others, spoke up and began bragging that they all should have been Euro nymphing as the Sexy Walz Worm tied behind the heavier Frenchie with 2mm tungsten beads was the ticket. Wearing a vest adorned with miscellaneous gadgets hanging in all directions, he looked like a gaudily decorated Christmas tree.

Before anyone else could get a word in edgewise, he continued explaining that he originally started fishing with Newbury's Dirty Hipster and a Blowtorch. Finally, after fishing hard and only landing a few fish, he decided to change his entire rig, add a longer Sighter piece, and four feet more of tippet. Then he changed flies to the Frenchie and Sexy Waltz worm dropper and caught fish consistently.

As he was catching his breath, preparing to continue his dramatic monologue, the heaviest and probably the oldest member of the group, known simply as Reverend, joined the conversation. His voice had an aura of fly fishing knowledge, assurance in his skill, and confidence that exuded from his persona. He looked like a man who had pursued trout his whole life.

Even his vest was different from the Kid's. His was tattered, stained, and floppy with pocket corners probably resewn by his own hand. Underneath, the armpits were split open and resewn with shoelaces. There was a fly holder made of string connecting old wine corks dangling down, all littered with flies and hooked on the same loop as his fingernail clippers.

"I noticed some larger Dark Hendrickson's hatching in the eddy when I first got here," Reverend recounted, "so I tied on a dry and eased up to them. I managed to catch a few small natives on top, and they really were acrobatic when they discovered I had 'em hooked."

"A size 16 dun caddis was hatching with lots of hungry fish feeding in a run above, so I eased up to them. The fish were splashy and feeding on the emerging pupa. This makes it tough to catch 'em sometimes."

"During this caddis hatch, I fished the X Elk Hair caddis in size 16. When I tie that fly, I loop the poly yarn at the tail, add a twist to the bottom and spread the material out into a bubble. I tie a palmered, grizzly saddle hackle, clipped flush so it would lay flat across the water. Fish find it irresistible when caddis are popping out. Find a good piece of muskrat fur for body material, and use the dark portions to tie both these flies. It'll make a difference."

Reverend looked at Newbie and continued, "I tinker with flies and take a good pattern, add or subtract things, and then catch fish."

As he talked, he pulled a scratched-up aluminum box out of the top vest pocket jammed with what seemed like a hundred flies. He fingered through them like an Osprey looking for an injured fish and handed a fly to Newbie.

Newbie stood there holding his new fly, totally absorbed in the conversation.

The other gentleman, who they called Forrest, grabbed the flask and took an unusually large gulp as if trying to finish the liquid refreshment. With a slight grin, he politely turned, handed the almost empty flask to Newbie, and told him to enjoy it.

Examining the fly intently while taking a baby sip of liquid courage, Newbie began questioning the older gentleman as if he had just made a new friend.

"So dun is actually the color of gray and not referred to as mayfly adults?" Newbie asked. "I always thought there were only nymphs and adults, and now I discover there are emergers too. That's a lot of insects to imitate. I will never learn them all. How do I know what to fish? This is more complicated than I ever imagined. And now all the different fly names! I have fished hard all morning and caught zero."

They could tell there was a hint of frustration in his voice.

"What do I fish with now? How do I even know what to fish with?" he repeated.

One of the less talkative fellows, Forrest, finally turned back toward him and spoke while magically revealing a third flask at the same time. He politely offered Newbie the first sip and instructed him to pass it around. His threadbare vest pockets were bulging with assorted fly boxes, pill boxes, and anything else that could hold at least two flies. His rubber Red Ball waders had a dry rot, inner tube look. They'd been mended with tire patches in several places but still held strong.

"Learn how to read the water well, and don't get caught up with all the hyperbole and jargon junk," he said gruffly. "Trout get particular from time to time but are opportunistic feeders overall. Just concentrate on understanding the currents and where the fish live, then get the fly down to them drag-free."

Reverend and the Kid grunted and nodded in agreement while the flask was double-dipped several times as it was passed around in circles. Newbie felt as if he was developing a true kinship.

The sound of squirrels rustling in the branches above woke Newbie. He had stopped to eat lunch and the music of the river lulled him into a peaceful slumber. A thick bed of moss shaded beneath a towering hemlock invited a quick snooze. As he woke and began stretching his stiffened muscles from the morning wade, he realized dusk was approaching, and it was time to head home. What a great afternoon nap, he thought.

As he lay there and pondered the day's events, there seemed to be a sense of clarity on how to fish the river and what he needed to do to catch fish. He thought about every detail of his dream and wished it wasn't a dream at all. As he talked with the men, it seemed as if time had stopped. He would have loved to stand in cold water, fish alongside those old guys, and become a part of their circle of friends.

As he squeezed his hand shut, something pricked his palm. Opening the hand, he found a sweaty bit of elk hair wrapped around a number 16 hook. The fly, he thought?

He smiled, arose, and walked around searching for evidence of the others, only to find one set of bootprints on the sand bar below the boulder. He grinned and gently laid the fly in a rusty, old aluminum container he noticed half-buried beside his fly rod.

Even though he left the river without catching a single trout, the river gave him a gift that would prove its worth in days to come. And that made this a great day, after all.

The Cure for the Fish Itch

Have you ever had a severe case of the "fish itch" - when the itch to go fishing is so bad that the thought of fishing is all-consuming? And scratching won't be the cure, either. It begins with an occasional memory of past fish and trips. Then it mushrooms into thoughts about fish you probably should have caught but didn't, lost by either tactical errors or equipment failures. It happens.

Fishing scenes multiply in the back corners of my mind and slowly consume me. The fish itch often gets to the point where it can drive me to think about it all the time. To adjust my mindset, I must go fishing to release the itch or struggle and try to ignore it.

If the fish itch affliction goes unattended, my body may undergo fluctuations in blood pressure, heart rhythm, and anxiety, and body temperature can range from hot to cold, relative to where my imaginary self may be fishing in the adventure.

The fish itch may begin with thoughts from a tropical setting. I am standing in clear blue saltwater and white sand with summer temps or feeling a western cold front and surrounded by snowflakes in a Montana stream, watching midges hatch like kernels of popcorn. There is always that extraordinary experience within each trip that I yearn for again. Sometimes, I cannot quit thinking about what causes me to have the fish itch constantly.

Every fisherperson has one of those moments. You look down and imagine the fly rod in your hand and start to move the arm back as if to recast. The knuckles are tight with the empty, cinched fingers. Then you suddenly realize that it's time to fix the fish itch quickly. Solving the puzzle and releasing the anxiety the fish itch is causing can be problematic. The diagnosis is simple.

For me, the fish itch can usually be temporarily handled with a fly-fishing trip somewhere. I try to move on to the diagnosis and prescribe a new adventure as quickly as possible when afflicted.

Apprehension can make the fish itch almost unbearable. Should I go? Maybe or maybe not. Then I think about what projects or honey-dos need to be done beforehand, check to see what's on the schedule for the next day, and then ponder some more. Procrastination does not bode well when consumed with the fish itch. I once went ninety days without fly fishing. I became so overwhelmed that I would stand in front of the sink and just feel the cold water running over my fingers.

The power of suggestion can explode a fuse and light a fire during this time of fish itch distress, especially when a text from a friend creates a nervous and uncontrollable fish itch tension. I had thought about going fishing but didn't pursue the thought too deeply. When the text came through and stated, "Winds are dying down tonight, the lake should be flat," it began instantly.

The recent excessive rains in the foothills of the Blue Ridge Mountains caused high water in the rivers and forced me to think lake thoughts. Then, the text about "no winds" came in. There is no choice but to focus on fly fishing the lake. Striper fishing at night seems to be a portrait taking shape on my easel.

As I tell my wife I am thinking about fishing tonight on the lake, the conversation follows pretty much in this order.

"Honey, I'm thinking about hitting the lake to chase some stripers with those new flies I tied up this morning. They look so good I may bite one myself if I don't go fishing."
"What?" Then there is a moment of silence and hesitation, coupled with a look that insinuates I may be crazy.
"Do you know how cold it's going to be?"
"Yes, low in the mid-20s, but we'll be fine." As the conversation continues, I realize that any hesitation that I might have had about going fishing has disappeared. I wasn't really looking for approval but instead actually talking myself into this fishing trip. She had verified I was crazy years ago.

Then, I state the scientific factors to close out the deal and justify my fishing existence while making a futile attempt to satisfy any procrastination that may be trying to interfere. I express and share my knowledge, "The barometric pressure is about perfect. All four wind apps state the breeze to be three to four knots. Perfect. The moon is a waxing crescent and will set around 9 . P.M. A dark winter evening with plenty of stars. The next front won't come in until after lunch tomorrow as more rain approaches by the weekend. Better go tonight while the climate window is open."

I had just coerced myself into the trip and arranged a time for my friends to meet me, hook up the boat, and begin a new adventure. With a fatherly tone, I reminded them to dress warm!

The itch has me in total control. The best time to fish is whenever you can get away, but there are those moments when the "fish itch" helps to bring it into reality at a much quicker pace, and regardless of any outside influences.

As I pulled the boat out of the marina and looked west on that particular night, dusk was spectacular. Had I not gone fishing, I would have missed this magnificent sunset. Outdoor adventures always generate special visual moments that define each outing, and I felt honored and lucky to witness this. It may cause a fish itch at a later date.

With the navigation lights and GPS ready and functional and a quick safety check, we are headed down the lake to big water. Stars reflected in the mirrored stillness of the lake. It resembled a glass tabletop. I almost felt guilty about creating a wake in the presence of all this tranquility. No reason to hurry. Just enjoy the cold ride, drink my coffee, anticipate the fish bite, and appreciate quality time with some of my fishing family. I was indeed scratching my fish itch now with both hands.

On nights like that, sitting in the boat looking up at the cathedral of stars, I occasionally catch a glimpse of a falling star, hoping my wish for a giant striper is fulfilled. The coffee smells better as I open the thermos to pour another sip, making my warm breath denser in the chilly evening.

The fishing action was slow, but we managed to break off several fish with my new fly pattern and finally did catch a few nice ones. Tonight was not a numbers game regarding fish but a cure to stop the fish itch.

When the itch strikes, there is no guarantee the fish will bite, the wind won't blow, the river won't rise, or the fish will feed. But at least it helps the hesitation when other life factors try to cloud the fishing judgment of a fine outdoor adventure.

Deer Stand Fishing

Time passes at such an incredible speed. It's been 20 years since I ventured into the deer woods with a rifle in hand. I have always loved fall fishing, cooler temperatures, the beauty of the tree colors, and the water dimples caused by leaves filtering into pools and eddies. I replaced tree stands, rutting bucks, and grunt calls for more river serenity. It was a priority decision.

Time to break the fall fishing tradition for a weekend and spend time outdoors with my son-in-law on his family property. He has waded rivers with me and chased fish on the fly from the mountains to the coast. Now, it was my turn to enjoy his world for a weekend. His passion for deer hunting would rival most. Today, we would split up our passions: a morning deer hunt and an afternoon pond fly-fishing trip.

Thirty minutes before daylight, I climbed up the ladder to make myself comfortable in a box stand constructed of 2x4s, 2x6s, and plywood, situated about twelve feet off the ground. My full coffee cup and a light jacket were in order. A comfortable and cozy 48 degrees with air moist enough to see your breath was a reminder colder temperatures and winter would be
approaching soon.

A quiet stillness prevailed. At the early hint of daylight, a pair of barred owls broke the silence. I occasionally listen to them from my back porch at home. There is something special about being surrounded by acres of wildness and hearing their voices echo.

The deer stand was situated near the edge of a swamp and a longleaf pine thicket with enough hardwood trees loosely scattered to break the monotonous pine outline. This location also afforded me the luxury of listening to wood ducks leaving the roost for their morning flight. My coffee tasted so much better out here. Sitting quietly and motionless would be nearly impossible, and I was glad to be encased in this wooden box perched on the pines' edge.

Without the normal interruptions of civilization, I could sit and mentally plan my annual Smoky Mountain fishing adventure coming up in several weeks. Sitting there quietly, almost trance-like, I couldn't ignore the activity of so many small songbirds dancing along with the weeds and bush-hogged walking path below the stand. Buntings, chickadees, and wrens were nervously flitting around directionless as the sun began to peek over the pine tops.

Several birds landed on the roof of the deer stand, scratching the tin sheet as they walked overhead. One bird decided I was lonely and flew directly into the deer stand with me. What a commotion commenced! The flapping of wings and bird feet in my face created a high degree of anxiety for both of us. Successfully surviving an upset songbird bird "close encounter" is a remarkable feat.

After this event, I surmised that every deer within hearing distance had been spooked. I had a little coffee left to drink and picked out the floating feathers. After twenty years, I had forgotten how stressful deer hunting could be. Time to get back to thinking about my fishing trip.

The heavy, damp morning air created condensation on the inside of the tin roof. Gravity worked well as these tiny droplets echoed a heavy thud as they splattered the wooden floor and the back of my neck.

I looked at my watch and realized I had been sitting here for more than an hour and hadn't thought about my upcoming fishing trip. Being mesmerized by the dawn's awakening of wildlife just enveloped me. Then I heard a cluck, a soft yelp, a cluck again, and here they came. The turkeys arrived like a marching band at the Macy's Thanksgiving Day Parade. All nine hens were clucking, yelping, and scratching in single file, a resounding cacophony announcing their presence and pecking order. They appeared to be headed to a small disced-up patch of ground to the east of the tree line.

I had forgotten about the quiet mornings in the deer woods alone and was totally enthralled with these awakening moments. Time had stopped, and I was caught up in the idea of just being there, visually watching the wildlife show as it unfolded.

A pair of squirrels gathering acorns in the oaks began barking, chattering incessantly, and scurrying up the tree. They wouldn't shut up. They were totally focused and fussing at something.

Movement from behind caught my eye. Four skinny trees in the thicket were connected and had a tail that swished from left to right. A small buck stepped out, raised his head to sniff the air for danger, and then began crunching acorns as if purposely aggravating the squirrels. The buck was cautious and, after a few minutes, quietly faded back into the thicket. Several does tiptoed across the field's small clearing and showed themselves briefly, also fading back into the loblolly forest thicket.

I never planned the Smoky Mountain fishing trip, and the world didn't end. I even failed to raise my gun. The box of bullets had been left on the coffee table in the cabin, and it didn't matter. What an awesome and eventful morning. Time to go pond fishing!

Back, One More Time

"Never knew a man not to be improved by a dog." Robert Ruark

The fire tinted the entire cabin with a warm but tender glow. Orange and red coals smoldered below the grate as the oak wood splintered itself in the flame and crumbled through the metal that held it up. The wind howled with a viciousness outside the thin, wooden walls.

Occasionally, one could feel its presence moving the flame of the kerosene lamps to one side. A symphony of sleet and freezing rain pelted the tin roof as if trying to penetrate the barrier between us and nature.

I got up from the chair to shuffle my boots around the fire screen to prevent them from burning. They needed to be somewhat dry for the next morning's hunt.

Dinner had been a filling and simple one. Spending all day in the elements tends to make one hungry but a little weary of going the extra mile for some fancy cuisine.

My hunting companion was asleep now. She lay fully extended on the brick hearth, warming her cold and stiff back. She moved somewhat slower now. The heat appeared to loosen her muscle cramps and release some of the stiffness. A muffled grunt of contentment sounded when I reached down to rub behind the ears, and a sigh as she rolled over. We were both getting much older now. She had aged more gracefully than I.

We both had enjoyed too many fine meals and it showed. My weather-beaten face exhibited lines of crow's feet around the corner of my eyes, along with tarnished skin subjected to the elements one too many times.

Her face was marked by a grayish, white distinctive fur against a black background. She had a set of loving, saggy brown eyes whose affection for me impaled my heart. The soft, warm flicker of the fireplace and kerosene lamps turned the mood into one of pensiveness and somberness.

The outing had been a welcome expedition for two old-timers feeling squashed by modern civilization. This trip was also marked by both parties' melancholy mood of mystique. Though a sound had not been spoken to her, my hunting partner and I both instinctively knew this was our last hunt together as a team.

We would always jump ducks, hunt pheasants in the wheat fields, and scan the sky for the occasional dove whirling and twisting on a northern tailwind. When we do these things again, it will not be on this plane as we know it now. When we meet again, my every shot will count and her every retrieve will be marked and retrieved with confidence that only experience could bring.

The rum seemed warm as I raised the tin cup and sipped in her honor. I sat back in this old rocking chair made of applewood, propped my feet on the table, and began to reminisce about my loyal hunting companion and our adventures.

This old cabin had been my institution of reverence for at least sixty-five years that I could remember. As a boy, I had hunted ducks, woodcock, and grouse in these woods with my father. It symbolized a place of special inequities that could only be found here among family and friends during the many past hunting seasons. Not everyone was invited to our socials.

Dad had said there would always be two prerequisites to handing out invitations. First, there must be love and admiration for nature and all her accolades that abound around this tiny cabin. Secondly, there must be appreciation for the many fine hunting dogs which have been kenneled here. These included a pack of setters, several pointers, two Brittany spaniels, and finally, my loving Labrador.

When walking in, her first woodcock retrieve is mounted on the knotted pine paneling to the right of the main cabin door. I need to dust it off, but no one can see how old and feather-worn it has become in the fading light. And this damp, musky cabin odor only embellishes the mood of those times gone by.

As a puppy, her willingness to investigate new surroundings was utterly amazing. Barely two weeks old, she followed her nose and sniffed around the garage, studying all the new smells. I watched her crawl across the floor, knowing that life to her would be one exciting, fascinating and continuous retrieve. She would inch her tiny black body on the cold pavement on a discovery mission and later sniff her way back to momma.

This gentle, cuddly little pup had distinguishing markings and noted tufts of white fur underneath her front paws. The only time the white would show was when held up to be admired or later as an adult when she held out her paw to shake your hand.

During the next six weeks, I remember spending hours watching all the puppies develop and establish their unique personalities. There was always this one puppy that would interact with me and eventually break off to romp on new adventures. I knew the white tufted feet pup was going to be mine. This pup sensed it belonged to me too.

With every visit, the entire litter would playfully greet me. As with small children, their introduction was always brief, except for this one little black anomaly. She sensed I would lead her into new surroundings and endeavored to follow me around the yard. When she tired, my shoe became her pillow, and she would plop her head down there. I rubbed her gently, and she sighed back lovingly. A bond had been established that would span a dozen years. This loyalty was never to be doubted and was always met with a wagging tail. In my eyes, a great hunter, retriever, and canine friend was beginning to reveal herself.

Bringing her home to the family and spoiling her was half the fun. Sometimes, in the early morning on our first daylight walk, I would sip on my coffee and watch her chase bugs across the backyard with a stern determination. After this tiresome pursuit, she would wag her whole body back to me for a pat and brief rest. I laughed when she clumsily staggered up the deck steps in a drunkard fashion to join me.

I knew that one day, her coordination would carry her to new heights of respectfulness and admiration in my eyes. I hoped that she would soon have a growth spurt and grow into her feet.

When her formal puppy training began, her first retrieve was astonishing. The nylon dummy was thrown about fifty feet away. Her intensity and speed coming to me almost landed her in the next county. She ran by me with so much energy that I thought she would never stop.

In the proceeding eighteen months, she matured and realized her true calling in life. The first dove shoot we were invited to participate in the following year revealed a marked improvement in her training and retrieval finesse. She no longer retrieved everyone's birds and brought them back to me. This time, she sat squarely to my left and began to look skyward. Without looking up myself, I could tell birds were flying by her whimpers of excitement. She had a way of looking at me with those big brown eyes that revered in disgust and shame at my missed shots and opportunities. I humbly would beg forgiveness and rub her behind the ears, and all was well again.

During long periods of boredom on the dove field, when the birds would sit in surrounding trees and mock the many hunters in camouflage, she would become restless and eventually put her head in my lap for some minor entertainment and patting.

Several months later, we would begin a tradition of many duck seasons. Together, we would wade and confront whatever nature threw at us regarding rain, freezing temperatures, and frozen precipitation. Wood ducks, mallards, and teal usually filled our bag limits when the elements were right. It didn't take her long to learn how to swim through the maze of decoys that lay anchored in the marsh. Dragging seven or eight magnum CarryLite decoys with counterweights around served as a good reminder not to entangle herself while retrieving.

There were lean years too. Times when the huge flocks we once watched come down with the Jetstream from the northern prairies never stopped here. It was the companionship and camaraderie that made the hunt. When this happened, we would amble back to the cabin for a quick meal and return to chase woodcock and grouse instead.

The alarm clock rang with its usual intensity. She heard it first and came over to see if I would turn it off and nuzzled me in that direction. I had slept hard sitting in the chair. These old, creaky bones took a little longer to get where they were headed. The cabin had really cooled down. A few coals remained, smoldering in the ashes of what had previously been a comfortable fire. It did not take long for my priorities to be arranged accordingly. I lit the lamps and started the fire one more time.

My companion sat idly by the door, scratching for a brief look at the outside weather. The wind had finally calmed, but a bitter chill enveloped us. Several inches of new snow quilted the earth with tufts of white. Icicles dangled down from the tin roof, while tree bark appeared shiny with a slick covering of sleet. All was quiet except for the crunching of snow below her feet. This blustery weather appeared to invigorate her and renew her desire to hunt. She sensed excitement would soon be here with the approaching dawn.

I gathered my gear and grabbed one cup of coffee for the hike ahead. It was hard to be somber with the adrenalin flowing. Together, we hiked down the trail as we had in years gone by. Her acute awareness seemed to interject a feeling of peacefulness. As we approached the marsh, she readily began swimming across the frozen surface, breaking the newly formed thin ice sheet. She had been here before, and I just followed her watery trail. I crashed around and managed to disperse a few decoys to make the hunt interesting, but my desire to ascertain a bag limit was not forthcoming.

I climbed into the blind made up of marsh grass, old pallets from work, and handfuls of cattails. Their iridescent hue of moisture prismed in the arrival of a new day. A few remaining gray clouds hovered and spit snow, but the sun would prevail. As the tip of its rays beamed across the sky, woodies flew from their roost in the mighty water oaks around the bend. Their twisting and turning revealed a flight path that did not include this frozen marsh. I reached down to pat and gently rub her behind the ears. Her once wet coat was now illuminated with frozen diamonds of ice against the black fur. Her whiskers sparkled with a heavy buildup of dampness from hard breathing.

Looking down, realizing I needed to make this hunt memorable, I decided to make one shot count and only subject her to one retrieve. We watched flight after flight of mallards disperse into the lake just a few miles beyond. Occasionally, I would call to them, but only half-heartedly. I knew if we waited, soon a small flock would fly the marsh edge, and just a few notes from my old Chick Majors call could work magic and might turn them to us.

Her head turned from side to side, intently focused on the sky. She shivered involuntarily from the cold with an occasional whimper of discomfort. We both waited. I finally called several small flocks, which showed no interest in joining their plastic friends in front of us.

It was evident the weather was hurting my companion. As we stood to move from the blind and head back to the cabin, a pair of mallards surprised us with wings cupped and orange legs outstretched, preparing to land in the decoys. Our movements immediately spooked them, and I raised my gun, only to lower it slowly and watch them fly out of the swamp. We both knew it was time to leave. I rubbed her head and quietly realized I would never say "back one more time" to her ever again.

Fishing Friends

"Bragging may not bring happiness, but no man having caught a large fish goes home through an alley."
~ Author Unknown

My Fishing "Family"

"One thing becomes clearer as one gets older and one's fishing experience increases, and that is the paramount importance of one's fishing companions." – John Ashley Cooper.

One of the greatest fishing experiences in life is not always a journey to some predetermined exotic fishing destination or landing that trophy fish to be photographed and released for bragging rights later in time. It's about the people you fish with and the many adventures you all enjoy together throughout the years.

Besides sharing the sport with children and grandkids, sharing trout waters with the same guys for almost 40 years or more is quite an accomplishment in itself. To be lucky to have such a long history of fishing friends can be loosely defined as a fishing family and encompass an endless list of stories.

There is one exception, however. We taught a "young" new Trout Unlimited member to fly fish during a local outing 23 years ago. Today, he's still affectionately referred to as the "Kid."

From marriage to children, hospitalizations and illness, career path interventions, life's tribulations, high water, hurricanes, flash floods, shark encounters, and sea sickness, and now the addition of grandchildren to pass these stories down to, our loose group of fishing friends remains very close. No matter what life would throw at us, there was always one resolve: just go fishing and continue searching for the next adventure.

Everyone is still healthy, able to fish, and has somehow managed to survive all the "low budget" but fabulous excursions we have taken throughout the country chasing fish.

Floating the West Branch of the Delaware River at extremely high water with individual pontoon boats and laughing as the frothy white water whipped us quickly down the river, few (not many) fish were caught. An aging memory can only think of three total during the rapid ride down the river. We had hauled the boats for 15 hours, frames stacked high in the back of my truck, from South Carolina and were determined to use them, especially since the water was too high to wade. But that's how fishing trips go. If there is high water in New York, then drive south to Pennsylvania!

Camping trips involved sleeping in vehicles, leaky tents, sleeping on picnic tables, and in a car dealership lot because it was thought to be safer and certainly cheaper, than a motel. We remembered to leave early before the dealership opened. Another attempt to save every extra penny to buy fly-tying materials and equipment.

It's not the fish that we remember first, but the events that encompassed the fishing experience. We made journeys to chase and catch fish, and these events surrounded that experience, but all the other non-fish-related experiences dominated our conversations during fishing family get-togethers and outings.

Driving 21 hours in 1981 to Baldwin, Michigan to catch salmon in the Pierre Marquette and Baldwin River. Driving straight through and getting out of the car and jumping directly into the river instead of checking in and resting for a few hours. Going from 10-to-15-inch trout in South Carolina to 10-to-15-pound chinook salmon in Michigan was nothing but a pure adrenaline rush that could only be cured one way: by hooking salmon. After fishing all day, I remember that first night in Baldwin. It ended early.

We drove through parts of Colorado one fall week, trying to fish as many Blue-Ribbon waters as humanly possible in six days, despite the heavy snowstorms. We fished dry flies during a blue-winged olive hatch on the Colorado River while the snow decreased visibility to mere feet. Not to mention that one in the group started a sing-along at the Laughing Ladies Restaurant in Salida, Colorado with an emphasis on Johnny Cash songs.

One year an Enterprise van – probably manufactured and designed to haul school children to special events, which explains the academic discount we received at the rental counter – was driven for a 12-hour journey to Mountain Home, Arkansas, to visit the White River. The fishing was excellent, but the stories revolve more around the karaoke sung at a Mexican restaurant.

It's hard to forget that rendition of the Allman Brothers' "Whipping Post." Several patrons didn't stay long enough to get their "To Go" boxes. Later, at the hotel in Cotter, Arkansas, there was a sign in the bathroom that read, "Please do not clean fish in the sink!"

During another trip, one hotel proprietor was so proud of the new mattresses that were recently purchased that he made a point of coming around to all four of our rooms, wanting to know how comfortable they were, seeking some form of reassurance of his investment. We happened to be gathering outside the rooms to head out fishing when he walked up.

Of course, one family member then mentioned that, indeed, the mattress was comfortable and that his wife wanted a new mattress, and what kind did he recommend? The proprietor then explained that he had gotten a good deal from the Holiday Inn across the road as they were changing theirs out. He then gave my friend the phone number and contact information. Needless to say, ours were the only four rooms rented out that particular week.

Some stories include fishing till 'dark-thirty' because the fishing was so good – with wild fish sipping dry flies during the evening hatch – then remembering that we didn't grab a flashlight and the truck was three miles back through the woods. Thankfully, if we walked by or over any snakes, we didn't see them or they just didn't feel like biting.

We understand each other as to what type of water each likes to fish, such as pocket water, runs and pools. And we know not to leave our fly boxes unattended in the truck, as it is customary to be filched by the others. It is also a tradition that we torment each other like brothers on the river and tell the same fishing story repeatedly in five different variations during times of excess libations. Seems each time a story is told, the fish count changes along with their size, but it really doesn't matter. The intervention of cell phone cameras has quieted some of the braggarts when a witness is not around for verification. However, there are still times when a witness can be bought and coerced using adult beverages.

There is an inherent admiration for each other and our various fishing abilities. All of us tie flies, but within the group is a spirit of individuality in trout fly perspectives and the way we see flies and tie them, which makes this such a great sport and hobby. All are excellent fly tiers and even better fishermen.

One fellow's fly box looks surreal, with flies neatly stacked and proportioned according to hook size and color. Each fly box contains a toothpick to pop up flies from the rubber tacky. The flies he ties are delicately balanced and proportioned and require extreme patience and skill, along with good eyesight. I admire his flies and love to raid his fly box when left unattended. That's what the backseat on trips is for.

I've also tried to emulate his organizational skill with my fly boxes and even went to the extreme of using a Sharpie to write on the outside as to their contents. Finally, I had to purchase another fly box and just wrote on the outside, "Surprise Me." My fly box toothpick was used after the first shore lunch I packed.

Another fishing brother believes in tying only sparse flies. Each fly had barely enough material to cover the steel hook. "Old-timers tied sparse flies," he would say. We always thought he didn't want to purchase more materials to tie with. He tied them with natural materials such as fox fur, muskrat, groundhog, squirrel, and dog clippings from his wife's groomer. He kept giving her zip-lock baggies to use after she swept the floor between canines. Yet he is a true fish-catching matching machine, so I cannot argue with his sparsity.

It doesn't matter with whom we share stories, and our fish always grow in size, girth, and stature in the stories to our non-fishing friends. It is incredible how fast a fish can grow within two hours of catching and releasing it. But exaggerating the size of a fish is not a lie. We decided many years ago that fish could always be bigger if flattened, fileted, or squashed by a truck tire, so why not go ahead and figure that length in also? We fly fishermen tend to look at fish through two eyes; one eye to see what fish and how we caught it, while the other eye sees how big we really want the fish to be.

The legal advisor in our little group developed an outstanding definition for this concept. He states that "a fish-related exaggeration is not considered a lie but merely a slight nonintentional overstatement of facts that occurred during a time of high excitement, which could then blend the many visual memories into one." This definition helps me to sleep at night.

Since 1978, we have trudged through many rivers, taught each other new fly patterns to tie, fished new places, and shared life experiences, but most of all, we continue to have fun and share a long-lasting affection for each other, our families, and the fish that brought us together.

Minnows, Children, and Crayfish

Growing up in rural Greenville County, South Carolina, the little houses sat together but were still somewhat secluded and surrounded by trees and woods. What an excellent place for young boys to grow up and enjoy the outdoors. The entire section of the undeveloped woods became their backyard.

The forest was littered with imaginative, secret trails and paths leading to various creek sections that ran lengthwise through the neighborhood. Of course, there were forts built of fallen logs and sticks and hidden with pine needles as camouflage. Age, engineering, and rainy summers forced these secret hiding places to be built above ground versus in old ditches, which carried copious amounts of water and became rather muddy during the storms.

In the back of little boys' minds were always the thoughts of ghosts, haints, and hobos that walked these woods at night. Little boys' logic determined it was better to play in the woods as a group, especially when dusk approached.

Three little boys called this neighborhood home. Being of the same age, they bonded and played hard in the woods during summer breaks. Each day gave them the opportunity for new discoveries and adventures and reasonable attempts to behave themselves.

Rivers, Alex, and Henry enjoyed many wonderful summers tromping these estates. The thought of adulthood began around the age of eight, and each was slowly granted more freedom to wander further in the woods. They explored, built forts, and fished for tiny bream that lived in the deeper pools of the creek. It was a wide creek that meandered and snaked along the entire undeveloped subdivision.

During one outing, they found a nice pocket of water that had eroded the ground under the roots of a rather large oak tree. The little current had washed the sand away, and a cluster of small rocks and pebbles were perfect ambush points for the crayfish. Using the meat of a bologna sandwich, they realized these crayfish could be coerced into attacking and latching their claws onto the bologna, which was dangled by the shoestring from one of the boy's sneakers.

Their minds began to churn and filter ideas about catching more crayfish with less effort and not ruining their sandwiches. After much discussion, an idea emerged. But they would need supplies.

Finally, they decided to go back to Rivers' house and look for the necessary materials. His dad spent a lot of time doing yard work and probably owned the most "tools and stuff." First of all, a burlap bag was needed. Several types of bags were discovered, but burlap seemed the best choice as water could seep through but still hold the critters about to be caught.

Rivers' dad kept extra lawn fertilizer double bagged in a burlap sack tucked away in the shed located in the back of their lot. Through their combined efforts, the heavy fertilizer bag was dragged from the inside out into the grass. The contents were emptied onto a nice green patch of fescue. Since they were going to be using the burlap bag, it was also decided to fertilize River's backyard as payment for the sack. Handfuls of fertilizer were scattered, dropped, and piled in little mounds throughout the carpet-like backyard of fescue.

A sense of pride overwhelmed them. Instead of just taking the bag, this act of responsibility demonstrated to their parents that an eight-year-old was indeed a grownup after all. Surely, this excessive fertilizer would make the grass grow faster and greener. Rivers' dad would indeed be proud of their efforts.

Rivers grabbed the burlap sack while Henry took two bricks from a pile of stone next to the shed. Alex grabbed a hoe and off to the creek they went. Once there, a careful study of the plan was reviewed and rehearsed several times.

They realized a container was needed into which they could empty the bag's contents. So, they decided to grab a gallon jar from Alex's pantry containing his dad's pickled eggs. They grimaced at the stench from the vinegar as the contents of soft eggs and liquid were dumped next to the trash can. Now they had the perfect container to hold their new treasures.

Once arriving at their appointed destination, Henry placed two bricks in the burlap bag, one in the back to hold it steady while the other was placed near the bottom opening to keep the current from closing it.

Henry stood thigh-deep in the pool and held the top open as water ballooned the sack. Alex stood above the current, took the handle of the hoe, and began jabbing it violently into the hidden watery cavern underneath the oak. As the handle descended deeper into the dark hole, he called Rivers to stand behind him and grab his belt in case something unforeseen began pulling back on the hoe.

Since Henry was the only one who would open his eyes underwater, he took a deep breath and submerged face down in the pool pulling the submerged debris into the sack. His job was to ensure all contents floated inside and the bricks stayed in place. During this time, Alex continued to aggressively poke, push, and wiggle the hoe handle deep inside the submerged tree roots, stirring the water into a muddy soup while Rivers knelt behind him, tugging his belt and saving his life from any disaster or encounters with trolls.

By the time they finished several rounds of poking, probing and catching, 40 good-eating-sized crayfish were stacked and crawling in the bottom of the glass jar with pinchers arced for combat. Catching crayfish was a team sport that provided a sense of accomplishment and satisfaction.

Time to head home and show their parents this fine catch. Upon arriving at Rivers' house first, they realized it was only noon, and the fathers wouldn't be home for quite a while.

Food was an afterthought, and besides, it was time to build another fort further up the creek. Ideas and thoughts of eight-year-old boys were constantly changing. Alex left the jar on the top brick of the planter, beside the azaleas and summer flower garden at the edge of the patio. It would be in plain sight when they returned, and they then could show off their prowess.

They returned near supper time and ran over to show off the pickle jar and its treasures. To their amazement, the soft gray shells of the crayfish had turned bright red with pinkish hues around the edges. Three young boys were sorely disappointed when they discovered their prizes had boiled and died in the hot sun. It was decided they would go back in the morning and repeat the gathering.

In the meantime, something had to be done with the dead crayfish so they could reuse the pickle jar. Henry, stating he was the most mature one of the group and being two months older than the others, offered to take the hoe and be responsible for the crawdads' burial. He promised each would get a proper sendoff and knew of a damp, cool area where to lay them down. He came back later and showed the clean jar; mission accomplished. All tools were laid outside on the ground near the shed, ready for tomorrow's task.

It was about three days later, while working on the worm farm that Rivers' dad walked up to the boys and mentioned a fishy smell coming from the back of the house. He said it was permeating the sheetrock walls and seemed to be getting worse. The hot, dog days of August heated up everything, while the attic fan pulled in muggy air and smells inside from all the opened windows.

While playing in Rivers' room, the boys surmised the stink was their summer clothes from all the tasks of building forts, caretaking of the worm farm, catching creek creatures, and just plain ole sweat. The longer the days passed and the hotter the outside temperature, the more the smell permeated throughout the entire house. Rivers' mom got lathered up fussing about the stench and thought about going to see her mom out of town until the problem was resolved. She even refused to use the attic fan until the problem was identified and fixed.

An exterminator who was called to search the house finally found the source of this fishy asphyxiation. After he left, the other boys' parents were called over into a joint conference. The kids hoped that a beach vacation was being planned, so they were excited to sit in on the discussion.

Being red-faced with angry scorn, the fathers seemed quiet as the boys entered the room. As a group, the mothers always sat off to the side whenever the boys got into trouble and let the fathers do most of the talking. The moms would always collaborate and negotiate lesser sentences of restriction later when everything cooled down. This time would be no different.

After heavy discussions, the true story slowly emerged. It seems that Henry had laid all forty crayfish neatly underneath the crawl space beneath Rivers' house. Four rows of ten were lined up neatly, with claws forward next to the concrete block wall of the crawl space entrance. He had successfully created a crayfish cemetery. The boys were quietly proud of him.

On the wall above the crayfish, written in chalk were the words,
      "Here lies our crawdads
      The sun-baked em red,
      The fish wouldn't eat them
      So we put them here dead."

The more Rivers' father talked, the redder he got, reminding the boys of the dead crayfish in the pickle jar. It took about a week, but he finally forgave them all. Rivers and his mom went north to visit his grandparents until the stench finally cleared. In the meantime, Alex and Henry kept the worm farm growing.

Crickets Big Fish

"Fill your life with experiences, not things. Have stories to tell, not stuff to show". ~ Unknown

Are all fishermen liars, or are we just encouraged to make profound statements about our catch and then be forced to back them up? Stretching the truth about a fish's weight, girth, length, and duration of struggle is not considered a lie by fishermen in my fishing group. Despite any unwieldy struggle a person interjects about catching a fish in their fable, I always sincerely want to believe them when they tell their story and hope they believe me when I tell mine.

Am I gullible? No. But I have stories of my own and can fabricate them quickly. I listen and find others' tales interesting and educational. Maybe there is part of their story I can use later. Fishermen are not liars, just creative people who like the outdoors and can communicate their achievements and disappointments extremely well.

But there are those nonbelievers who don't trust what we have to say. They are a small crowd of folks who need proof or want to challenge the story. Cell phone cameras have helped substantiate the truth in stories. Unless it was left in the truck so as not to get ruined or waterlogged. That makes perfect sense to me, and the stories continue. I happen to believe them all. It's less stressful that way.

Here's a story that required extreme professional circumstances to be proven. Even the substantiation part is a story in itself.

Not long ago, I had the privilege of accompanying a friend of a friend's nephew on his mother's side fly fishing. It seemed like the young man, named *Cricket* Davis, had a burning desire to try his hand at fly fishing. Always eager to make fly fishing introductions to young folks, I agreed to meet him at an appointed destination and time. And being a friend of a friend's friend, I thought the day would go extremely well, coupled with his high expectations.

Finally, the planned day arrived. We met at the appointed location and began to "wader up." I had previously asked if he needed any equipment, and he emphatically said 'no,' as he had borrowed some gear. Evidently, his wading shoes were too small, so he literally cut the front toe portion off, leaving three inches of naked neoprene booty sticking out, ready to meet stream rocks personally. I knew from that moment on it would be a day to remember. I wish I hadn't accidentally left my cell phone at home; otherwise, I would have taken a picture of his feet. I guess I could have borrowed his phone to take a pic of his protruding toes and texted myself, but that wouldn't have looked professional.

Geared up, rods connected, and flies tied on, off we went. As we walked the path, I couldn't help myself; I had to ask how he became known as *Cricket*. Seems he had been using the little critters to catch bream and sent the hook straight through the cricket and into his index finger past the barb several years prior. Cutting the monofilament from the hook eye, he wandered around the pond, trying to find his buddies for help. Finding them, he extended his finger, revealing an embedded hook with a cricket kicking frantically to free itself.

He said the first thing they did was laugh, then began taking pics of his circus finger. No sympathy was shown whatsoever. Had I been there, I would have videoed the jumping cricket. He mentioned it was quite the round table discussion on extraction. I suspect it was shown on social media also. One buddy pulled out his pocket knife, ready to cut off his finger and save the poor cricket.

The hook was finally yanked out with monofilament and the cricket died. The nickname *Cricket* has stuck with him ever since then. He wanted to learn to fly fish but couldn't find anyone to take him. He thought it would be a much safer and "cleaner" way to catch fish.

In the back of my mind, I wished I had prematurely asked more questions about *Cricket* before I agreed to take him fishing, but we were ready to go and determined to make the best of it.

It was quite the afternoon. He was a natural and listened attentively with a willingness to learn. We caught some nice trout. Catching and releasing several in the 12-15" category taught him how to fight fish on the fly.

As the afternoon waned, *Cricket* eyed one last upstream area he wanted to fish before we left. We eased up there and caught a few fish before landing a very nice rainbow on his last cast. I took pictures for him, and he thanked me for hanging with him.

The next day, my phone rang, and it was *Cricket*, still excited about that last fish. It seemed like his friends doubted his newly acquired fly-fishing prowess and his version of the story. Evidently, pictures weren't enough to verify his catch. Unbelievers again rose to the occasion. He asked me if I could assist and give him some kind of certified written statement about the fish and the trip.

Pondering the thought, I decided to call one of my retired buddies, who is a Notary Public and could certify my statement. For a bottle of liquor, he could be persuaded to sign anything. I composed a few paragraphs about the day I spent fly fishing with *Cricket* and bribed him to notarize my signature. I hoped this professional document would quiet the masses on his achievement and shed some truth about his big fish.

Below is a copy of my sworn statement.

I, Mike Watts, do solemnly swear on the life of the first buck I ever shot that the following statements are true and factual.

On Saturday, April 15, 2023, *Cricket* Davis was fishing with me in a secret, cold mountain stream located off a two-lane road in the mountains of North Carolina. During the morning session, I watched him effortlessly hook, play, and release several nice rainbows in the 12-15" category. I could tell by the way he lifted the rod tip at hookset on each fish that they would be hooked in the upper corner of the mouth—true poetry in motion. If I remember correctly, I called them "ESPN" moments as my net slid like a grease fitting underneath each of them for a quick release.

It was around 2:00 in the afternoon, and I just finished drinking a Dr. Atkins Power Drink and snacking on a low-carb power bar. I know the exact time, as I was starving and had looked at my watch, thinking about the Dairy Queen we would pass on the way home. My wife had put me on a diet and refused to cook anymore until I lost 15 lbs.

The previous night's rain stained the river somewhat but began clearing up nicely after lunch. *Cricket* kept eyeing this one long run ahead of where we were presently fishing. Watching the water tumble over a small waterfall, creating nice riffles, he finally couldn't stand it anymore. He had to fish it, and I just humbly followed behind. I tried to keep up with him, hastily racing to the "Spot." The pace at which he was wading reminded me of the Daytona 500 last-lap finish. Unable to keep up, I was prepared to lag and net him if he slipped, fell in, and floated by.

Once there, he quickly picked up two nice fish in the 15-18" range. They fought really well but were no match for *Cricket* and his 4X tippet. He had called his "riffle," and it produced well. But he wasn't through catching fish yet.

After these fish were released, he changed flies and wouldn't show me what he had just put on. I knew it was one of mine that I had previously given him because he didn't have any flies of his own. This was to be called his new secret fly. Holding the fly in his lips but not getting it stuck showed fishing maturity and experience. He used both hands to create some type of special saltwater knot, tying the tippet with the size 12 woolly bugger in his lips. I was watching *Cricket* history being made, quietly preparing to call 911.

With laser focus, he rollcast effortlessly, as instructed, to the river's top right eddy and held his rod tip high, bringing in all the slack. This was like watching an outdoor fishing program with no commercials. I was in awe of how quickly he had learned.

As the current drove the nymph underwater, the fly line jerked back violently, and Cricket lifted up. Some form of river monster began to thrash, and *Cricket* reeled up the extra hand-held fly line and confidently eased down below the fish. For the next 10 minutes, maybe longer, a fight ensued, with *Cricket* slowly gaining back the fly line. When the fish jumped, it reminded us of a submarine surfacing with its enormous body. Then, it peeled his flyline off quickly as it attempted to find a way up the small waterfalls. Impressive, *Cricket* knew exactly how much pressure to apply and when to apply it. It was a textbook display.

He barked at me to ready my long-handled net and stand beside him. Being somewhat weak from lack of nutrition on this diet and lack of food, I was hesitant to stand in waist-deep water with that fast current but I wanted to see this trophy fish up close and personal.

I made three attempts to slide my net underneath this behemoth before success. On each net miss, *Cricket* barked instructions in Southern English. He was now the captain of this ship. I feared for my life if I broke this fish off with sloppy netting.

"Fish head's up," he yelled at me. "Net now, go underneath the fish quickly before he gets caught in that other current!"

I followed his instructions and rapidly lifted the fish up. Without hesitation, I was as worn out as this fish was. That Dairy Queen would see me shortly.

Finally, success! We stood there admiring this magnificent trophy trout. High fives and a few loud "Yeah Babies" were in order. Then, of course, it was picture time. I begged *Cricket* to take my picture holding "his" fish for bragging rights with my buddies but with no luck.

With his left hand, he gently held the fish's head into the current, watching the gills move, slowly at first and then gathering strength. Its tail rode the current, swaying back and forth until it finally flicked with a massive kick and swam away.

I had goosebumps from excitement watching the show and the confidence of *Cricket* as he hooked and landed this monster.

There should be no reason to doubt any of the facts stated above. According to my memory, this is a true and accurate account of this day. The day my new friend, *Cricket* Davis, landed the big 'un.

Witness Signed: Mike Watts. Signature_______________________________________
05-01-23

Notary Public: Seamore J. Hooks Signature _______________________________________
My Notary has Expired.

For Everything There is a Season

"Come to the woods, for here is rest." ~ John Muir

Fall Fishing in the Smokeys

"Come to the woods, for here is rest." John Muir

The fall is a brilliant time of year to fly fish rivers for many reasons. The streams throughout the Blue Ridge Mountains of Appalachia once again come alive with hungry fish and a beautifully colored landscape. Cool nights lower the stream's water temperature, and trout emerge from their lethargic summer state to a more active one, especially when it comes to eating my fly.

Summer months are spent streamside at daylight wade fishing, hoping for a couple hours of solitude and just putting my feet in the cold, running water. The hope for a fish fades when innertubes appear, with their occupants splashing and laughing as the sun warms the water and air temperatures climb to their summertime highs. But it's all right to share the river for now. They'll be gone soon enough.

By noon, my summer fishing usually comes to an end. When the dog days of August are in seasonal control, my thoughts turn to fall in anticipation of all the fishing this season has to offer. And when the first cool nights of late September finally appear, with night temperatures in the 50s, excitement reigns.

During the fall, my fishing days become longer, and I observe leaves slowly fading from green to red, yellow, and orange as time passes. I quietly wade the same river edges I did in summer, but now, serendipitously, I find hungrier, rising trout as I fish my October caddis pattern. My imitation brings an occasional strike. The water is usually still low and clear from summer but is beginning to turn colder again. Except for occasional remnants or deluge of a tropical depression, the rain doesn't usually pick up enough to restore water flows until mid-October through November.

Everyone has their favorite fall stream, and I am no different. I have become nomadic to a degree and want to fish them all. Early fall in the Great Smokey Mountains is a special time. Being at a higher elevation, fall begins to settle itself here first.

Several Smokey Mountain Rivers come to mind when reflecting on my fall fishing experiences. Fishing the Oconaluftee, Raven Forks, and Cataloochee Rivers can be exceptional, along with their feeder creeks. Small, native rainbows caught fishing dry on a three-weight rod while listening to a bull elk bugling, trying to round up his herd of females, never ceases to send a cold chill. Once, I walked up on two young bull elk sparring for dominance while standing in the run. I had wanted to fish. As I eased down the path, my movement caught their attention, and they surveyed me intently as I quickly hastened along. A management decision was made not to argue with them over that run but to wander and find another.

Each season brings a different temperament to a river. The moods of a fall river are more reluctant to offer a fisherman a few fish when compared to summer. With water levels still low, the fish became extremely wary and spooky. I remember sitting on a moss-covered bank and watching a pool above me. The older I get, the more I like to sit and observe. There were some feeding fish in the pool, but when the gentle breeze from an approaching cold front caused acorns and twigs to thump the water's surface, they scattered. But only briefly.

Another stream I fish meanders down from a mountaintop spring, runs through a small gorge, and funnels over a waterfall. From there, it flattens into a slower-moving river. One year, I had worked my way up to the waterfall and found the perfect rock offering me a place to sit and have lunch. The woods are usually condensed with trees, with little sunlight penetrating through the summer canopy. But on this fall day, I couldn't help but admire the variety of colors that seemed to brighten the woods.

The intense colors of the yellow and orange leaves appeared to absorb the sun and radiate the hillside with light, brightening the forest of evergreens. I remember that small hoppers and larger Adams parachutes worked well that day. Those feisty, wild rainbows pulled hard and jumped with intensity. Pinching down the barbs allowed for easy releases.

Being on the river in fall also brings a sense of solitude. Football and hunting seasons have filtered most of the anglers. Except for the leaf watchers and ardent hikers, the river's wild occupants and I share an uncrowded experience. Remnants of walnut husk lay heaped in small piles as raccoons bring them to the river to wash before devouring them. Abundant animal tracks embroider the riverbank, leaving indentations of prior visits.

The fall air has a clean crispness to it. The haze from summer humidity that enveloped the mountains has now left. It feels exhilarating. And the fish seem to like it too.

Dealing with falling leaves can be aggravating but only briefly, usually lasting just a few weeks. If leaves were fish, I would consistently have spectacular days fishing. When my flies finish their drift and begin to swing around, they become a leaf magnet.

Dead leaves are always attracted to my hook point. Pulling them off before the next cast becomes ritualistic, though it becomes a chore after a few hours. When several leaves get hung at once, they bend the tip nicely. It's the larger poplar leaves that provide some of the greatest resistance. Just a small sacrifice to find that willing fish. There are moments when the fish caught are so small that compared to the leaves, the leaves pull harder in the current; they just don't get acrobatic.

Watching a fluttering leaf catch a slight tailwind and glide down to the water is peaceful. Small dimples circulate outward as it gently and silently lands on the surface, and the water begins to wash it downstream. And onto my hook.

Cloudy days account for tiny blue duns and blue-winged olives appearing, offering some dry fly action. Scattered caddis and midges hover over sunlight-warmed pools.

Fishing never stops in the Blue Ridge Mountains, but fall is a special time. It stretches from short-sleeved shirts in September to fleece and flannel in November. Every river has its own distinct mood and personality, and I will continue to always wade through the changes. There is something special about the fall. However you define it, "happiness is where the heart is."

Teenage Turkey Dreamers

Spring is a time of fishing rods, barefoot in newly cut green grass, short-sleeved shirts, baseball, and the sound of songbirds returning from their migratory journey. It is a wonderful time for teenagers to raid their worm farm and march to the local pond to bream fish.

Spring is also the time for turkeys. Hearing the mating ritualistic gobbles of the tom turkey will make a person squirm with excitement. During this time of year, various imitations of vocal commands from hen turkeys can be heard by everyone who pursues this favorite Spring pastime.

For three teenage boys passionate about the outdoors, patience is a hard lesson to learn. Turkey season needed to get here faster. Anticipation of the hunt and calling to turkeys were the most important thoughts in their minds.

Their attempt to make turkey sounds echoed high-pitched, spine-tingling, and screechy when they tried to imitate a hen calling out for love. Two of them had homemade calls made of old chalkboard pieces with a whittled hickory sapling carved into a striker. They were determined to imitate and learn a turkey's vocabulary and be able to communicate with them.

School in spring was a lethargic time for these three best friends. They possessed a burning desire to romp across and throughout the turkey woods instead of sitting in a classroom looking out the windows and thinking about it. Patience was not an adoring virtue for them.

These three boys practically lived from one hunting season to anticipating the next one. Spring was a special time. It allowed them to use pent-up energy stored during bitter winter days and provided excuses to procrastinate on schoolwork.

Their fathers hunted together in a club called "The Big Hoof Sportsman's Club." It was a grand place extending over several thousand acres with all the hunting rights leased. Plenty of acreages for grown men to be boys and boys to be boys. Plenty of room for riding four-wheelers on dirt roads and camping at the old log cabin. The focal meeting place was the big fire burning inside a tractor hub, providing every man and boy a place to spit. It was the centerpiece of all congregation activities and deep discussions. Acting responsibly earned the boys permission from their fathers to hunt turkey by themselves this year. They thought it was time to graduate from boyhood to manhood. Doing so made hunting this spring an honored privilege.

After much thought and discussion, a turkey hunting plan was developed and approved by their fathers. Rivers, Henry, and Alex laid out the blueprint of a special turkey hunt on opening day. They would leave early that morning, skip school, hunt, and be back from the "hoof" about the time school was out but in time for baseball practice. Perfect, they thought.

Rivers was to be the head turkey caller. His dad had shot a few birds over the past years, which elevated his level of expertise, and he had been watching his dad's instructional VHS videos. His dad had also bought a few low-budget calls, ranging from mouth diaphragm to slate calls for him to use, which sounded much better than the old homemade ones. He practiced along with the videos, calling back at the television set, and was turkey-yelping at every chance.

Around the neighborhood, one could hear Rivers yelping in the background. He identified with the turkey, and his head jerked every time he called out. Neighbors were amused at these incessant head movements. Every "yelp" appeared to imitate a chicken pecking for bugs.

Each boy had a task to complete before the day of the big hunt. Henry took charge of the turkey scents. Each wanted to smell like a turkey; as they had read these were such wary birds, and they thought every advantage was needed. There were no references to turkey smells in any hunting magazines, so he finally surmised that if deer could smell, then turkeys could smell too.
Wilbur Armstrong, a farmer, lived down the road about a mile from Henry and owned a turkey farm. Collectively, they ventured down to the farmhouse and got permission to see the turkey pens. There, Henry began to develop his premium turkey scents, custom-made from the real thing.

Rivers began bragging about the sweetness of his calling, and the other two boys decided to call a bluff on his technique. Rivers slightly opened the pen door, and out flew two beautiful white butterballs. Once they cleared the ridge and were out of sight, the boys listened and hid in the boxwoods near the pen door. Rivers pulled his new slate call and began sending screechy sounds while Alex and Henry laughed.

Suddenly, two white objects appeared like ghost turkeys, clucking loudly as they crossed the ridge back toward the pen. Speechlessness and awe described the moment. The birds would have never spotted them had it not been for Rivers' head violently jerking as he hit the call's striker vertically across the slate. They all agreed it was still a very impressive showing for Rivers. Now more of a reality, constant dreams of a magnificent, wild gobbler appeared in their heads with its' tail fully fanned, strutting and drumming, showing the other forest creatures he was the king of spring.

April 15 was most significant as it began the opening of turkey season. Now, three teenage boys didn't have to be sneaky and harass any more of Mr. Armstrong's turkeys. By the time turkey season had arrived, they had quite the bone pile of shot turkeys hidden behind the turkey pen woods with all white, feathered evidence buried. This practice helped them determine the yardage required to pull the trigger effectively and which part of the turkey to aim for.

It was again cleared from a parental viewpoint to proceed and let the boys go alone and responsibly to the "hoof" to chase turkeys on opening day. The plan was to take Henry's four-wheel-drive jeep. Besides just turkey hunting, there were always mud puddles to cruise through, firebreaks bordering cutovers to ride around, and other neat places to scout and trample in. Henry had a winch on the front bumper, so getting stuck and walking back to the cabin for help was unimportant.

Opening day was finally here. Daylight was less than an hour and a half away and time for the journey to begin. Several miles out of town, a sudden spurting noise under the hood alerted them to the possibility of an imminent delay. At first, they thought Rivers had swallowed a diaphragm call he purchased the day before.

However, it only took a short time to realize they had forgotten to fuel up the jeep in all their excitement. Now stuck in the middle of nowhere, out of gas with a jeep full of guns, ammunition, food, and turkey calls, there was only one option left.

Since it was Henry's jeep, it was only natural for him to volunteer to find fuel. Reluctantly, he proceeded down the dark, lonely road alone with only a flashlight and an empty red gas can.

Surely, somebody would eventually pick up a scraggly teenager strolling down a county road holding only a gas can. They all hoped the flashlight batteries would last until civilization was found.

Meanwhile, Rivers sat in the front seat and practiced imitating the voice of a forlorn hen incessantly. Finally convinced to be quiet, Rivers and Alex decided to settle down, crack the windows, turn on the blinkers for safety, and snooze. They knew that when Henry returned, their quest for this elusive gamebird would be theirs.

It seemed like only minutes before the sound of logging trucks and other vehicular traffic awakened them, and the light of dawn appeared. Alex shook Rivers front seat to wake him, and they clamored out. There was no sign of Henry anywhere. The sun was beginning a fresh new ascent with nothing but barren woods and forest engulfing them on both sides of the road.
The "hoof" was their planned destination, but these woods sure looked inviting to two overly anxious and bored teenage boys. It seemed to be calling their names to enter.

Several "Posted" signs had been shot through and were rusting, peeled back, and almost unreadable. They thought if a sign was deemed unreadable, it had no meaning, and they could enter the beyond. A note was left for Henry on the windshield. The storm drain was muddy but easy to cross. Surely, this new frontier would have a few gobblers close by.

Once across the culvert, Rivers was asked to sound off his array of hen calls. Alex leaned against an oak and listened intently as Rivers decided to use his slate call first. His "Stradivarius" squawked, "cheok, cheok, cheok," breaking the stillness of daylight.

The boys started walking and followed an old logging road beside the ditch as it ventured towards a ridge. From that vantage point, it was hoped his turkey sound would echo into Sir Gobbler's ears who would answer back with a resounding gobble. If this technique worked on the turkey farm, it would surely work in these big woods. As Rivers continued to walk and call, Alex urged him to cease with the neck dancing. Too much movement, according to Alex.
They had developed a master plan to avoid getting lost.

Every few yards, Alex would take a piece of toilet paper off the roll and drop it on the ground. When it was time to exit, they merely followed the double-ply trail back out. How ingenious, they thought.

It would have been perfect, except for the rain that fell the night before. The ground was still saturated, making the double-ply soggy and almost invisible within minutes. After hiking around for thirty minutes, the boys were in a dilemma. They had walked the entire ridge top and two bottom areas, were out of toilet paper and realized they were indeed lost. With each step, a soggy slushiness broke the quiet stillness of the woods. Suddenly, they noticed how heavy their boots had become with mud caked between the vibram soles.

They reluctantly trudged forward, lost and now hungry, except for an unwrapped Snickers bar Alex had stuffed in his pants pocket. Most of the chocolate was melted and replaced with pocket fuzz and whatever else had been there before. It still looked appealing to two hungry teenagers. Rivers commented to Alex that he would owe him for the rest of his life for saving him from starvation.

Out of nowhere came a deep voice," You boys lost?" Rivers and Alex were aghast. They thought out loud, "Has God found us?" They looked so puzzled and were readying themselves to run when an apparent bush-looking creature began to stand up and walk towards them. Whatever was left of the candy bar Rivers held was squeezed into a marble-sized ball of chocolate. They were so shocked by the apparition they became too scared to run. Their minds were already over the ridge, but their legs remained motionless.

This apparition moved towards them at a steady gait, and as it neared, it began tugging at its head, and off came a camouflage mask. Underneath revealed an older gentleman with a crinkly face.

The boys figured the lines marked years spent outside weathering the elements, and age. There was a piercing kindness in those squinting blue eyes. As he approached, he again asked, "You boys lost?"

Speechless, both heads nodded back and forth in the yes motion. Before the conversation continued, Rivers and Alex knew they were in the company of a great Sage and needed to show respect and reverence. Too bad Henry didn't check the gas level before leaving town, as he would have truly enjoyed this adventure.

They began explaining to this gray-haired gentleman their dilemma of running out of gas early morning, waiting on their friend to return, and that they didn't know this was private land since the posted signs were old and shot up. Their shotguns were carried for protection purposes only.

The Sage laughed amusingly and asked if they had seen anyone leaving traces of toilet paper on the ground everywhere. In the same breath, he also asked if they had heard any toms gobble in the early morning, to which they both emphatically replied, "No." Sage instructed them to follow him and would lead them back to Henry's jeep.

As they walked, Sage never made an introduction but instead began pointing out a turkey sign to them. He explained the difference between hen and gobbler tracks, the different droppings of each sex, and the dusting places these birds regularly used. The boys fired question after question and were answered in a soft and knowledgeable tone.

Rivers and Alex immediately became experts with this new knowledge and couldn't wait to share it with Henry. As they neared a small rise, Sage motioned for the boys to stop all chatter and unnecessary movements. They bent down, crawled over to a large pine on the edge of the logging road, and leaned against its rough bark. Rivers sat to Sage's left while Alex went right.

He whispered for them to camouflage completely, rest the shotguns on their shoulders and prop the guns' forearms on their knees. Rivers whispered that he had left the turkey scent in the jeep and hoped they wouldn't need it. Alex reminded him to keep his neck still when he heard turkeys calling.

Within a few minutes of courtship yelping by Sage, a thunderous gobble exploded, and the throttling sound of the birds' drumming reverberated throughout the woods. The hair on their necks stood straight as these two boys embraced this moment. The expectation of actually seeing a wild gobbler was almost more than these young men could handle.

Sage whispered again that they should not move a single muscle. Alex tried not to swallow for fear of giving his position away, and Rivers had to concede and finally began to breathe and blink his eyes. He later confessed that sitting there so motionless made his nose itch and eyes water!

Minutes seemed like hours. It was as if time had stopped. Then finally Sage whispered, "Here he comes!" Rivers saw him first. The blood-red head of this regal tom wattles, shaking with every step as he picks and pecks his way around fallen logs, looking feverishly for the hen that had so lovingly called to him.

At that time, the camouflage hid the boys sitting and shaking with excitement, almost hyperventilating. Rivers also confessed that his heart had been beating so hard that he was worried about the gobbler hearing it.

As this grand gobbler approached, its tail became fully fanned, and its chest protruded forward. His long beard brushed debris from underneath its chest. They could hear it drumming, mixed with an occasional cluck. Then it would cock its head back and burst a mighty gobble which, in turn, would cause its entire neck and chest to wiggle while giving two teenage boys goose bumps.

The Sage sat there perfectly still. Finally, he whispered for them to shoot when the bird reappeared from behind a tree. The moment they had dreamed of, read, studied about, and longed for was becoming a reality.

Alex steadied his shotgun and sighted down the vented ribbed barrel, waiting for the bird to make this one last final appearance. He knew Rivers was doing the same. As the bird continued its search and stepped out, Alex held his breath and gently squeezed the trigger, only to hear the sound of a snap. The disappointing sound of a firing pin hitting an empty shell cylinder.

Two milliseconds later, Rivers' gun went snap too. Both old pump shotgun forearms were getting shucked back and forth quickly as they watched the bird putt twice and race back into the forest. They had forgotten to grab shotgun shells in their haste to venture from the jeep at dawn.

Both boys jumped up and began a tongue-thrashing dance like this stretch of woods had never seen before. They paraded around the tree, blaming Henry for running out of gas, not reminding them to bring shells, load their guns or anything else they could find wrong. They felt that if Henry had been more responsible, none of this would have happened.

The sound of traffic, logging trucks, and mufflers rode heavy in their ears. A loud banging caught Alex's attention and he sat up somewhat bewildered and amazingly lost. In the front seat sat Rivers, head laid against the glass, snoring and drooling down the jeep window.

Outside was Henry banging a metal gas can against the gas cap, refueling the vehicle and hitting his pocketknife against the back quarter panel, hollering for them to wake up. As Rivers began to come alive, he rolled around in the seat, looked at Alex, sheepishly grinned, and asked, "Who brought the shells?"

Serenity

The 4th of July is a difficult time for serenity and solitude on a trout river, the day being summer's most popular holiday. To find this peacefulness, I probably should have driven a little farther. The air temperature was a delightful 57 degrees driving across the mountains toward Brevard, North Carolina. I had no business driving to the mountains to fish this weekend. I knew from the beginning that I would have to share the river with flocks of folks wearing inner tubes and sandals, but I went anyway. Sometimes, I just have to do "fishy" things for peace of mind.

Several years ago, around this same time of year, I was easing down a river and noticed an entire family of five, somewhat sparsely clothed in waist-deep, cold mountain water, soaping up, shampooing, and bathing themselves. They had been camping nearby. I had been on a diet for about two weeks, just long enough that all I could think of was food and fishing, and I almost asked if I could go back to their campsite to fetch towels if they promised to scramble me a few eggs and hashbrowns for breakfast. Willpower ruled out that thought, and I turned back around to fish.

I really had no business being up here, but I wanted to fly fish this weekend. Instead of fishing, I could have been home doing yard work, landscaping, or painting the deck. I succumbed to my hobby.

The best time to find serenity and solitude would be early dawn. I left the house in darkness and drove across the mountains with headlights, watching the sun wake the world. I was surprised at the traffic on the roadway at this time of day, but it was a holiday, after all. Most of the human population in the U.S. is on vacation this week and probably camping near my destination.

I arrived and pulled off the side of the road. I readied my rod and flies and traveling light today, I only had a couple of fly boxes to carry. I had decided to do some wet wading, noting that July was the perfect month to leave the waders at home.

As I began to walk down the path to the river, I noticed a bag of trash lying below the automobile pull-off. I was reminded that not everyone has a deep passion for the outdoors like some of us. I picked up the plastic bag and put it in the back of my truck.

Easing down the overgrown path, I intended only to fish a specific 200 yards of river. If I fished slowly and methodically, a few native rainbows might bend my three-weight fly rod, and then I could drive back home satisfied, knowing the day was good. Mountain thunderstorms had been in short supply as of late, which caused the river to be lower than usual and clear as the drinking water at home.

I walked up the dirt path and decided to fish dry on top of the surface and also downstream to test my stealth. All fish eyes would be looking forward upstream and I hoped the audience would be pointing up towards the surface. Careful not to spook any fish, I maneuvered and stayed somewhat hidden in the tick-infested bushes and roll cast my fly line down and across.

This outing was already a success. No one was fishing in front of or behind me. These 200 yards of water were temporarily all mine. I fooled myself into thinking it was my very own stretch of private river. The ripples seemed to dance with the sunbeams and sparkle in the rising sun.

I crawled up on a log beside the river bank to sit, looking downstream for a few minutes, trying to inhale the moment. This piece of fallen hemlock must have contained a hollow core. When I finally positioned myself on it to enjoy the view, a nice black snake must have thought an earthquake was taking place above and decided to slip out quickly under my feet and find a more stable abode. It was time to bring out the emergency flask for a rather large sip of rum to settle my anxious nerves. I may be traveling light in regard to gear and flies, but there are some items deemed necessary. I was good as long as this creature didn't sound like baby rattles or didn't resemble a new copper penny.

A great blue heron flew into my pool. I wasn't really fond of sharing this morning, but I really had no choice. I hoped he was only lost and stopped to rest on his journey west back to the lake. He was a much better fisher than I. This was supposed to be my stretch of river, if for only a few hours. I would release my fish while he was looking for breakfast, but as his stalk began, I watched and began mine also. It would be Mano versus heron, and I had already eaten breakfast.

The last time I fished this section of the river was five or six years ago. History does indeed repeat itself. Some folks describe it as local knowledge, but I define it as age and experience. I will use the same "secret fly" today and the same size "secret fly" from years past. I know this because it worked before, and it is the only size of this particular fly in my box. I have not tried anything similar for the past five or six years. This shows that a person should never clean out a fly box, no matter how rusty the hooks.

The heron walked the water's edge with a precise purpose. Its neck was straining for flashes of movement below the surface. The flask and its contents helped to settle my nerves from the snake encounter. It was time to fish. The heron had the better side of the river with the foam line in front of him. Foam lines mean food to fish. Follow the foam and you will find fish; he knew that. Those long pencil legs of his went toe first throughout the water's edge and never made a wake. I watched him hunt intently. Now it was my turn. He seemed to ignore my presence.

I eased off the log gently and released any bark that I may have pinched in my cheeks during my sitting encounter with Mr. Snake. I should take some lessons and try to wade like a heron. We can all learn from nature if we just observe. Those big, clunky, felt-sole wading boots I was wearing were quiet but not like the gift the heron had.

Rings dissipated in the pool where the ripples flattened out. A trout fed there. I saw his lips when his head poked through the surface. I hope he didn't notice me and my five-year-old, rusted hookfly standing in the bushes above him. Was the knot good and would three feet of 6x tippet be sufficient to allow for a drag-free float?

One can only hope. I noticed my neighbor across the river had poked at several fish on the other side but with no luck. I eased out far enough from the bushes and cast downstream. The fly landed several feet above the last sign of feeding rings. There was ample slack in the fly line to allow for a short float over the target area, and then the fly would drag like a water skier behind a wakeboat. Totally unnatural.

Fish lips appeared and my flyline went taught. I gently raised my rod tip and slowly brought in a beautiful, wild rainbow. I admired the red-striped line and coloration of this wild masterpiece. I released the fish gently back into the water. As I released it, I began to speak softly to the fish.

He needed to know that I had waded these waters for more than 47 years and that his ancestors were as kind to me as he was. The day was a success already, and the fish just made it better. I cut the fly off and placed it back into my fly box. Maybe I won't wait another five years to use it.

The heron watched with a fit of intense jealousy. He saw the entire play be enacted. For 30 minutes after daylight, I proved to be the heron of that pool. They say that one can't teach an old dog new tricks, but occasionally, the old dog has a few tricks of his own!

Thanksgiving Trout!

The holidays are special times and should be a reminder of all things to be thankful for all year long. In most cases, they also offer a few days off for fishing trips, both pre- and post-Thanksgiving! This year was to be no different, except for the fact that I had a new fly fishing partner, my 4-year-old grandson.

The rain had been a scarce commodity in the mountains, and the rivers were low and clear. Perfect for a beginner to learn wading skills. I had to remember that my fishing buddy was barely belt high. Because of that, I could not fortress across the deeper holes but had to pick and choose parts of the river to stand with less current. Being a low-gradient river, sandbars dotted the bank, which afforded easier access in several locations. Clear water never looks deep and is deceiving, especially to the untrained wader. I had planned to keep him very close and physically carry all forty-five pounds of grandson to various eddies and sandbars once we began to fish. In case of emergency, I always had his dad positioned to lend a helping hand!

As he began to put on waders, I could tell he was excited about this new adventure. An enthusiastic twinkle in his eye appeared, along with an enormous smile. Unlike dressing for school, there was no argument about the fit or how different the waders felt. The waders were big but were the smallest to be found. I could have wrapped him in a waterproof cocoon if pulled up and over his head. It was my responsibility to keep the straps from choking him as they pulled down on his shoulders. I took an old military belt, cut off the excess and buckled him under the armpits. He was set to wade now. The walking pace to the river almost turned into an athletic event.

We had tied some flies previously together and cut the hooks off to prevent first aid measures. I tied a woolly bugger on the leader tippet, replicating the one that we had made weeks before and hoped he wouldn't notice the difference. This fly was on a barbless hook and ready to sore lip a few fish.

Last-minute instructions were given as we began to wade. Just like everyone, I have taken fly fishing over the years past, when wading a river for the first time, standing in the water and feeling the current pull begins a connection and affection to the river which I hope will last his lifetime.

"Papa, I'm not wet!" he exclaimed as he stood knee-deep and smiling. Then the parent in me had to remind him he would be soaked and cold if he didn't listen. The water temperature was noted as cold when he stuck his hands underwater and determined they were better off out of the water than in it.

I picked him up and crossed the river. Together we eased down the far bank to a run I knew possibly held a few fish and prayed for them to please eat the wooly buggar. Teaming up, we roll cast across the run and stripped the fly slowly as it entered the current. On the third cast, prayers were answered. I held the rod up with one hand and coaxed him with the reeling portion. Anticipation and adrenaline make a person of any age wind any reel as fast as possible so as not to lose the fish but indefinably, that becomes the end result.

The attention span of a four-year-old is usually only a few minutes, but I had his full attention and determination now. Maybe it's the pull of the rod that began the addiction, and it was time for another fish. Several more casts yielded a few strikes but no bites. We changed locations to a different sandbar and fished the lower run from a new angle.

Fish on and the smile continues. This time patience played a much larger role as he brought the fish in. Handing the rod off, he was determined also to net the fish himself. We had spent some time netting leaves in the water, and the concept of sliding the net underneath the leaf instead of "poking" at it seemed to resonate. As the fish's head was lifted, he became more focused and listened intently while gently sliding the net underneath the fish and lifting it up! Success at last!

Standing in chest-deep water, he stood there holding the fish with such an impeccable smile. Memories made on the river should last a lifetime. With a delighted tenderness, he revived the fish in the net and watched it swim off into the current. It was determined that wet sleeves and cold hands required some stream bank dry fun for a while.

Throwing sticks and rocks in water is an ageless pastime. Walking trails, running up the mountain and back down, answering inquisitive questions, laughing, and having a quick snack streamside top off an incredible afternoon. The fishing was great, but the fun the three of us had was greater. So much to be thankful for.

A Winter Fishing Dream

Christmas is over, and the new year is beginning. The collegiate national football championship is just a few weeks away, and Old Man Winter has a firm grasp on the weather. It's a good night to sit outside and build a fire. The cold front provided clarity to the heavens, and looking up, I could see all the stars without the haziness of summer.

The fire is popping from all the pine wood I cut up after the storm this fall, its red and orange flames crackling from the burning pine sap. The tractor ring encircling the fire pit is a reminder that old things are still useful. My front side is toasty, but my back remains cold, so I wrap the blanket tight over my shoulders and tuck the sides between my body and chair. There are no crickets, tree frogs, or cicadas to serenade the dark stillness; there is just a frozen quietness.

As I sit here chilled, my mind drifts off to warmer days of springtime. Casting a dry fly to a feeding fish is special. A gentle cast, then carefully mending the fly line, allowing the fly to drift effortlessly and appear unrestricted into a fish's feeding lane, tempting a pair of trout lips to break the surface and sip my imitation.

Staring into the fire and somewhat mesmerized, I notice the flames parting, revealing the stream bank flowing past a familiar sycamore tree. I know this place and have fished its waters for over four decades.

The sycamore's roots are firmly planted on the sloping bank, and the tree towers high and wide, guarding both the bank and the river. I have been here many times before. A deep pool extends out and is protected from the tree's lower branches. The shade from the limbs darkens the water and hides the inhabitants.

If I make a bad cast, the tree's big leaves seem to become a "fly" attractor and can be aggravating. I have lost many flies to them over the years. The riffle above the pool is shallow and a great place to cast. The slick, worn rocks reveal shades of tan, gray, burnt umber, and reddish clay. Many are loose and make balancing a chore when crossing through the swift current.

We all have our favorite places to fish, and this is mine. Closing my eyes, I can hear the river and its various melodic pitches of water gurgling and lapping over rocks. As I listen, it seems the river's shallower streambed has a higher pitch, while plunge pools resonate bass tones. Its runs, riffles and bubbly foam lines speak a welcoming language as if to say "hello."

Looking around, I notice several hemlocks have gotten tip-heavy and bent from the heavy snow in early January. I notice how thick the ferns have become along the valley path leading into "my" spot. Their light green leaves catch the indirect sunlight through the canopy floor and ignite the valley with an iridescent light green hue.

History and experience tell me that it's time for the little yellow sulfur mayflies to begin hatching and breaking the water's surface. I need to be streamside and ready when they mature. These small insects will transform from underwater nymphs into airborne adults and ride the current as their wings dry and become ready for flight, allowing fish an easy target.

The head of this pool is the perfect place for an ambush for both fish and man. Opportunistic large trout swim from the depths to the surface and feed on the vulnerable and abundant floating insects.

Standing in the riffles upstream, I patiently wait for the show to begin. Sporadic at first, the hatch appears, and so do the fish. After the first few sulfurs float through the pool, I notice a dimple in the slack water where the tree roots extend below the surface, offering protection and cover for the fish. Then another rise and dimple. These trout slowly sip tiny mayflies as they float into the back eddy an easy meal. The multiple currents and low, leaf-filled branches make a cast and drag-free float difficult. I don't want to take a chance on spooking the fish this early in the hatch, so for a few minutes, I stand still and watch.

Soon, little sulfurs begin to hatch with increased regularity. The surface appears like someone has poured a box of popcorn across the water. The fish begin feeding more frequently.

Then I spot him. A rather large brown trout of 20 inches or more. I've been accused of extending a fish's length and weight over the years, but with a sense of confidence, I know this is truly a nice fish. The trout feeds with an effortless rhythm. As the hatch continues to thicken, I notice his wake slowly and deliberately move to the head of the pool where the riffles tail out.

I quietly move upstream and off to the side to give my cast a better angle for accuracy. My old Hardy Princess reel and bamboo rod are ready for battle. I've tied the perfect imitation to replicate these dainty yellow mayflies with upright dun wings. The fish perches itself beside a small protruding rock and begins feeding. He continues to rise and feed with his upper body and dorsal fin, breaking the surface, submerging, and then repeating. My plan is to time my cast and have the fly float past him like a natural insect as he rises.

Intently focused, I gently send a roll cast about eight feet above the fish and softly throw an aerial mend upstream, giving the fly ample time to float naturally into the brown's feeding lane. The cast is perfect, and I know a hookup is mere milliseconds away. His body lifts with his mouth wide open, honing in on my imitation.

As my fly bounces in the surface film right into the mouth of this huge trout, the hookup and rod set are interrupted by a woman's voice, jolting me and forcing me to quickly and abruptly distinguish what reality is and what it isn't. She calls my name and throws a barrage of questions in rapid succession while violently shaking my chair.

"Are you asleep?" "Aren't you cold?" "You know it's getting late." "The fire is about to go out!" "Are you going to sit here all night and freeze to death?"

I guess I will never know if I indeed fooled that trout. Sitting there perplexed, I try to process what instantly happened. Awake and disappointed, I looked down and noticed my hand gripping an imaginary fly rod. It was almost like something was pulling on the other end. Smiling, I quietly think, 'Happy New Year to me!'

Christmas Magic

Christmas has always been and will continue to be, a special time at our house. Last year, I combined the perfect holiday with a perfect day of red fishing. Merging a festive occasion with a hook set into a saltwater redfish would add the finishing touches to this holiday. It was decided that the two of us would travel south to Charleston, South Carolina, in search of cooperating fish that understood our agenda and were willing to participate.

The weather was cold, with lows in the upper 20s near the coast but much colder as we left in darkness from the northwest corner of South Carolina. One of my longtime fly fishing buddies had agreed to join in, as we both had developed a severe case of saltwater redfishhookanosis disease.

The only cure was to stick a fly in the upper corner of several redfish mouths. To ensure our success rate, I decided to reach out and include my buddy of many years, Captain John Irwin of FlyRight Charters, also referred to as my resident expert. We have fished together for many years, and I consider him one of the most knowledgeable and personable guides along that part of the Carolina coast. Spend a day in the boat with him, and his passion for the resource becomes contagious.

Throughout the years, he has learned my casting strengths and weaknesses and patiently positions the boat so as not to expose them. During our previous fishing trips, he had explained many times these fish school up in big groups in the winter. He suggested I needed to experience this, as most of my redfishing involved chasing tailing redfish in warmer weather on flood tides.

When I called him about guiding us after Christmas, he mentioned that we needed to get down here quickly. He had consistently found them schooled in one particular area, and, of course, this played on my nerves. When a trusted guide buddy says to go fishing, the stars are lined up and it's time. Without hesitation or any second-guessing, I was obliged to make every effort to take advantage of this hot tip!

I had previously tied plenty of flies, such as the Purple Smurple, Gartside Soft Hackle Streamers, and Borski Sliders in various sizes, weights, and colors. On occasion, however, I have tied a box full of flies only to get to my destination and discover the fish have been hitting something else and are reluctant to bite my offerings. But on this day, it was to be different. Providence would be kind.

Careful not to overdress for the southbound caravan down, we arrived 3 ½ hours later in Charleston, a little before 8:00 a.m. As we crossed the main bridge over the harbor, someone in the truck had the bright idea to crack the truck windows and turn off the heat to "climatize" ourselves before our cold boat ride and excursion. By the end of the bridge, we had a change of heart and rolled up the windows. We would take our chances in the elements and test our clothing's so-called modern technology.

We met John at the landing, got an updated fishing and weather report, and readied the fly rods.

Soon, John was backing the small bay boat into the water, and two overdressed mountain trout fishermen were ready for action. One more Yeti cup full of coffee was needed for the ride.

Coats would come off later but were necessary for the bitter ride out to the oyster beds. After twenty-five minutes in the open air at 40 mph with the temperature hovering around 29 degrees, being overdressed was not an issue.

I was, as always, enamored by the marsh's beauty. Overhead, the clear sky was dazzling as it stretched across the boundaries of sight. The weatherman said visibility would be around 12 miles, but I thought I could see forever. Up close, blades of brown marsh grass swayed gently from the boat's wake. The mirrored water looked freshly polished, reflecting a rich cobalt blue. And there was a freshness to the cold salt air that was totally invigorating.

John shut off the engine as we glided around the oyster beds surrounding us. He climbed up to the poling perch, instructed us to get ready, and began to ease the boat along, stalking in a slow and quiet motion. He instinctively pushed us in and out of the oyster beds, each one growing as the waters continued to recede. In a few hours, the oyster beds would swallow us.

Shorebirds had begun to congregate on the drying oyster outcrops. A solitary heron poked around the corner, a pair of rails flushed as we entered, and several American Oyster Catchers ambled along a far oyster rake. The wildlife was active. If only the fish would cooperate now. It was their turn.

As we cornered a rather large oyster bed, nervous water broke the stillness and serenity of the moment and reminded us of our mission. The saltwater was so clear that small stingrays were visible, hovering in the sunny shallows, searching for a meal.

High tide was slowly depleting the marsh of water, which would set us up perfectly to hunt the shallows for the remaining salt ponds' indentations and congregating fish. The flats boat's design allowed us to glide across the shallows effortlessly. Years of experience allowed the 21' carbon fiber pole to be noiseless when gently picked up and pushed through the bottom soft mud and murk.

Fishing has a continuous learning curve with no payback for getting skunked. Each adventure is a new experience and provides a chance to enjoy the outdoors. A few hooked fish just make the experience a little more enjoyable. Over the years, I had my share of heartaches learning how to pursue these redfish, and being as it was Christmas, I hoped a few presents could be unwrapped or unhooked.

John called for the first cast to be softly dropped in front of the nervous water and to let the fly sink and sit, patiently wait, and then twitch the fly as the fish neared. My cast loops included high anxiety and goosebumps, but those were overcome by concentration and determination. First cast, precision, patience, twitch slowly, and a hookup! A fish well deserved!

Maybe this was all a dream, and I had indeed ventured back in time, and it was yesterday, after all. Either way, the day was going to be fun! During the next several hours, my buddy and I took turns and caught almost every fish John called out and some fish he didn't. Instead of captain, we should have called him coach!

I can vividly remember his encouraging instructions,
"Three o'clock, 40 feet…….. strip set!"
"Eleven o'clock 35 feet…….strip set!"
"Lock and load and stretch one out about 2 o'clock, twitch it, line moved, strip set! Nice!"
"Fish on!" was repeated after every command from the captain. Some days it pays to follow orders precisely.

After all the hard days and tribulations, lost fish, and the fear of being skunked while chasing these reds, our fishing Christmas gift had been unwrapped. Fishing that day with John at the helm, guiding, directing, and sharing his experience with my friend of many years was a blessing. Thoughts of "should have been here yesterday" disappeared and were replaced with wonderful memories of "fishing in Christmas past!"

Adventures & Stories to Tell

"The solution to any problem -- work, love, money, whatever -- is to go fishing, and the worse the problem, the longer the trip should be." ~ John Gierach

The Browns Canyon Adventure

The Arkansas River runs for 1,400 miles from Colorado to Oklahoma, across Kansas and Arkansas, before entering the Mississippi. One of my long-time fishing buddies, George Campbell, and I had flown 1,500 miles to experience the headwaters of this mighty river firsthand.

As with any fly fishing trip plans, maps were closely examined with notes written as to where public and private property access points were located, and roads were highlighted in yellow. With those chores completed, it was time to tie some flies. Compound this prep with high expectations and long-range weather reports, and it was finally time to head west and fish.

We decided to begin our adventure near Salida and fish north to Leadville and the headwaters of the Arkansas River. We included a quick trip to Pike's Peak and a late afternoon visit to the famous Silver Dollar Saloon. We had collaborated for months and were exhausted from the overstimulation of internet research. Break time!

Previous experiences fishing in Colorado in late September brought flashbacks of temps in the high 60s one day and then encountering snow the next day, depending on elevation. Lucky for us, the temperatures stayed somewhat mild and very dry for the most part during our trip of eight days trying to imitate trout bums.

Local knowledge from the fly shop had pointed us to start fishing at Hecla Junction above Salida, as the river was extremely low and clear, which allowed wading access to the cross. This section of the river is known for its white-water flows and is a focal point for rafters and kayakers. But low water allowed us access to taste the vastness of Browns Canyon by foot and fly rod.

As we crossed the river and climbed up the far bank, I gazed down the river at its pristine persona as it carved through this uncorrupted and unspoiled maze of granite, canyon cliffs and boulders. It was as I had imagined, wild, clean, and beautiful.

Remnants of a once-active railroad provided empty tracks and a hiking path through this rugged terrain. As we walked, a keen eye was always scanning ahead in case we met any of the local wildlife calling this area home, such as black bears, mountain lions, elk and big horn sheep.

It was decided that we would hike several miles and then start looking for a drop-off point to enter the water. Behind the froths of white foam, situated in pockets behind the boulders where the currents were slower, we hoped to find willing, wild browns hungry and not overly picky about the fly they chose.

Once we left the recreation site in our rearview mirror, we saw no one. After deciding to wander upriver instead of down, the only sound heard was that of a raging river below us and our footsteps crunching gravel between the railroad ties. The breadth of where we stood and the history that came before us overtook our thoughts and discussions. No fishing trip is complete without a prior read on the history and its relevance to an area.

Eventually, we walked in silence, trying to inhale all that Brown Canyon had to offer, even before we began to fish. The deep blue sky held up an intense fall sun, which appeared to warm the earth one last time before being overtaken by gray clouds of snow and the winter solstice. Continuing our hike and enjoying the landscape confirmed months of planning and preparation that, indeed, we might be at the right place, at the right time.

It seemed that every inviting pool and pocket of water called our name. Resistance to fishing was hard, but we decided to be at least two to three miles above the recreation center before starting to fish, hoping to find those "untouched" fish that swam wild and ignorant of our feathered imitations of insects on steel.

After about an hour's hike, as the river made a hard turn left, George decided to climb down the 40-foot escarpment and bushwhack through the willows to a large pocket of holding water situated behind two large boulders that deflected the rapids to the center of the river. It was decided he would join me several hours later and walk the tracks until I was found.

Walking further around the bend, I saw human life approaching in the form of two kayakers playing in the swift currents, twisting and turning their boats in the white water. I could only imagine the river's strength when at full pool.

Ambling onward down the railroad tracks, looking for that perfect spot to begin fishing, grew difficult. The whole river looked inviting, but I had in mind to find a section of the river that had a long tail out below the rapids and provided easier access to an old man.

After about twenty more minutes, I turned around and faced back to where I had been, mindfully retracing my footsteps. The railroad tracks seemed to disappear into the massive rock walls that enveloped me, arid and beautiful, dotted with sparse, green pinion pines sitting on ledges and then willows revealing their yellowish fall brilliance along the riverbank. Looking up towards the sky reminded me of a large peephole shining light into a box surrounded by high rock formations.

A little further, and there was "my" run. A long, flat, and clear tail out from where the river turned and bent slightly and slowed. A great place to spend a few hours fishing thoroughly and enough shade on the far bank to rest and have lunch later. My perfect spot. I descended the short climb down to the end of the tail out. Looking down at the sandbar, I noticed rather large animal tracks, and again, I was reminded I was only a visitor playing in their backyard.

Dimples from small caddis flies hatching to adulthood dotted the water's surface as they dipped and danced and tried to fly erratically in the softer currents. The water was clear, and the fish spooky. I put a 16 gray Elk Hair caddis and trailed a size 20 nymph dropper. Roll casting both flies along the edge of the foam lines, a small brown appeared and sipped the caddis fly right before the current began to cause the flies to drag. The first Colorado brown of the trip!

I continued fishing the edges and eddies methodically and quickly picked up several more browns, an equal amount on both dry and dropper. Indeed, the long leader with small flies with a 6x tippet was the perfect combination. But nothing lasts forever. For a while, the fish seemed willing and hungry, but as noon approached, it appeared that I became the only creature hungry.

Crossing the back of the tail out, I headed for shade, a wrapped-up biscuit from breakfast, and a Power Bar. The water was cold, but the sun was intense, and the surrounding rocks seemed to absorb its heat. Laying in the shade of a willow, thankful to be here, I watched the first two fly fishermen seen all day walk down the tracks looking for their fishing destination.

It wasn't long before my buddy came up, crossed the river, and shared my shade tree. Comparing flies, fish stories, and the excitement of being in Browns Canyon for the first time made all the planning and anticipation worth the effort. And this was only day one of our eight-day adventure.

After our shore lunch, we noticed several dimples from feeding trout appear near the head of the run, which signaled time to fish again. As I turned around to grab my pack and fly rod, another visitor quietly appeared and wanted to share my shade tree too. On a rock perched above us, a rather large bull snake, estimated at six feet long, had evidently just finished lunch as well. I quickly decided to let him have my willow tree shade and catch some rising fish on a dry fly.

Little blue-winged olives hatched for the next few hours, and the fishing was spectacular. We both fished dry imitations in sizes 18 and 20 throughout the long tail out to rising fish, respectively and stuck some nice browns. Neither George nor I hooked any browns larger than 15 inches but we consistently hooked them fishing our favorite way, with dry flies.

As fishing slowed, we decided to cross back across the river and walk the track further up to enjoy the scenery and see new sights. Tomorrow would bring a new day and another section of the river, but for now, we just wanted to be here.

Meeting the River of Stone

For centuries, Native Americans called the river "Thronateeska," meaning "flint picking up place." During its discovery by Desoto in the 1500s it was referred to as the Rio Perdernales, meaning "flint" in Spanish, and its name was eventually translated into the "Flint River." I renamed it "Awesome."

The river begins in Atlanta, Georgia and runs free for more than 200 miles south through Georgia, where it meets the Chattahoochee River, forms the Apalachicola River, and empties into the Gulf of Mexico.

Before fishing a new river, I like to research with Dr. Google and learn something of its history and facts. Reading and discovering how this river drainage impacted Georgia and U.S. history only added to the anticipation of seeing it firsthand.

I was spending the day with an old friend, Kent Edmonds, on a fish-catching discovery mission. The weather would be perfect to wet wade, with high temperatures reaching the low 80s.

I was in awe, looking at the river from the bridge overhead, knowing that its path had basically remained unchanged for centuries. It was wide enough that kayakers, float tubers and fishermen could all have their piece of the river and not infringe on each other. This particular shoal had rivulets of water spread through indentations carved in the rock over time, creating fingers of riffles to be fished.

I wanted my introduction to the Flint to begin by casting one of Kent's well-known fly patterns, the Stealth Bomber. Of course, I had tied up an overabundance of them and carried a fly box full of assorted colors and sizes of the topwater foam-based fly. I was thankful they weren't weighted flies. Otherwise, it would have been similar to wading with a pocket anchor, causing me to sink if I stepped into a hole. Kent may have saved my life and didn't know it.

The light fog was lifting as we found a path through the woods and finally reached an open outcrop from which to start. It's interesting how a fishing trip can be full of positive or negative signs reflecting the day's outcome, even before the first cast. As we neared the river, being so focused on its beauty, the many riffles and runs cascading across a large mound of rock, we failed to look down and see the water snake at our feet. Thankfully, it wasn't a poisonous variety, reinforcing my "sign" theory that it would indeed be a great day.

Kent had mentioned that the first appearance could be deceiving as the bottom may look shallow, maybe one or two feet deep, but the river rocks contained holes and crevices where the native shoal bass hide and ambush prey. Native only to these three rivers, the shoal bass provides an explosive reaction to a top-water gurgling fly, becoming airborne once it realizes it's hooked and putting a nice arc in the fly rod.

Entering the shoals' edge, this first rocky run was bordered with short grass along the back eddy and looked extremely fishy. The water dropped off an outcrop creating a foam line turning left away from the grass edge, creating a nice inside pocket for my bomber. The first cast caused a rise and a miss, but the second was a hook up: my first shoal bass.

Casting six-weight fly rods made using the larger Bombers easier to roll cast and land beside or near the targets. With each hook-up, these fish made hard runs, leaps and surges that continuously brought chill bumps to an old man as the day progressed. I never tire of catching fish, even small ones.

The top water bite began to slow as the sun began to rise above the treetops. We both put on a lightly weighted damsel fly dropper behind the bomber and skirted both flies across the ledges from riffle to riffle. I eased around one crevice where the river created a deep angled slide, bubbling downward with some degree of velocity as it emptied out into the pool below. I was entertained by a bale of turtles taking turns swimming to the head of the pool and then gliding along the swift current to the back of it. I couldn't determine whether they were feeding or just enjoying recess and a free ride provided by nature. Maybe even swimming lessons for the younger ones?

Several nice shoal bass were caught during the turtle intermission, no doubt caused by me getting too close to the water's edge during their show. Each fish hit the damsel dropper. During the fish-catching commotion, the turtles finally realized I was a spectator and here only to fish. Quickly, they returned to their synchronized event.

Standing there looking around, trying to inhale my surroundings and the low humming and soothing sound of so many shallow riffles, I became enamored with a long run on the far side of the bank. It was bordered with big rocks and high grass and appeared especially deep. I reminded myself that I was here to discover and investigate. Basically, I convinced my inner fish that the grass was greener and the fish were bigger on the other side. It was time to completely dismiss and disregard the old adage of leaving feeding fish to find more fish. There is this innate urge always to see what's around the next bend. The mystery of what fish was next to be caught pulled hard at my soul, and this new run looked more inviting.

Moving deliberately across the river, trying to focus ahead while looking back to imprint which rocks I had actually stepped on to cross over, had become a habit due to lessons learned the hard way. Sometimes, intently focusing on the fishing ahead has caused me to forget the path that took me to them.

Wading and climbing over rocks to get to my destination rekindled flashbacks of the past. I recalled wet wading for smallmouth bass in the French Broad River above Asheville, North Carolina, years ago. Again, I was determined to reach the other side and visually paid no attention to my path. I managed to zig-zag, wade around deep holes, and cross over on rocks to get there, and it was worth it.

When it got dusk, I looked around, and all the rocks looked the same. The headlights were bright from my buddy's truck, and he was probably drinking my beer. With too many rocks, surrounded by deep water, and with darkness approaching, I put my fly rod in my mouth and swam back across. I learned a valuable lesson and never told my wife.

Intermingled with the shoal bass, we also caught and released bream and a rather large shellcracker. Fishing up an appetite, we found shade, ate a sandwich, and discussed the fish we caught and the ones we didn't. Though not extremely hot yet, the sun was intense, and the shade was a welcome respite. Our fishing discovery mission was successful, and we were thankful for the invitation and the opportunity to experience this wonderful fishery. I sat and tried to imagine the river as it was hundreds of years ago. It's still free-flowing, clear, and clean due to the hard work of many agencies and volunteers.

For the remainder of the day, Kent and I fished and climbed around to new areas. We found some deep holes, came across new runs, and caught fish. We basically fished with the same two flies all day, and I was glad because my bifocals were left in his truck.

Shark Bite!

The mysterious predator of the ocean is sometimes referred to as 'The Man in the Gray Suit.' The sound of its name can bring cold chills. Holler those words on a sandy beach, and swimmers, sunbathers and others retreat quickly from the water's edge. Movies about its prowess and appetite have done little, if anything, to reduce this apex predator from its pedestal. All of the above make it an excellent challenge for chasing with the flyrod.

Several years ago, it was decided that this could indeed be a great gamefish on the fly. The predawn was warm and humid, as most summer mornings are in Charleston, South Carolina. The sun began to sneak up as we left the landing and headed toward the mouth of Charleston Harbor. The small breeze would morph into high winds after lunch as the sun began to bake down.

Not many boats out this morning, and still probably a little early for most except the die-hards, whose fish adrenaline rush can keep them focused and attentive for days on end.

Daybreak, looking out at the ocean, is always mesmerizing to this old guy who has spent more than many years chasing trout in mountain settings. It's a special time, but every day at daybreak, going fishing is truly a special time. Because sharks are most active in low light conditions such as dusk and dawn, we wanted to be there on time for the action.

For once, the tide and wind apps were absolutely correct. What a beautiful morning ride. Wave height in the ocean was to be around 1.5 feet every 8 seconds, which was perfect. Not getting knocked around the boat first thing made mountain boys getting sea legs easier.

We stopped briefly in a shallow cove and threw the cast net for menhaden. Thankfully, the bait gods were gracious to us with a great sacrifice, and we filled the cooler quickly and headed out. Now, it was time for the messy part. We took advantage of this riding time, and two of us started menhaden duty, cutting the bait in half and keeping everything in the cooler. We also filled several mesh bags with the slimy, smelly, gutty mess. Using the onboard water wash, we first sprayed each other down and then cleaned up the boat. It was strictly a matter of priority here.

Anticipation and anxiety were at an all-time high. Thoughts about our potential quarry ran amuck through my mind. Did they really pull that hard and runoff line? Would this twelve-weight fly rod really be too much or too little? Was this mass of red and orange marabou feather globs I had tied on 6/0 hooks really going to fool such an intelligent predator?

Several shrimp boats were about a mile out, scraping the ocean floor. As we eased closer, the smell of their diesel engines replaced the salty air. We were careful to stay far away from the seining nets dragging behind them. As instructed, I chunked several cups of menhaden parts overboard and tied one of the bait-dripping mesh bags with a parachute cord. The chum line trolled slowly behind us about 20 feet.

Several pairs of dorsal fins quickly broke the water's surface behind us. Chill bumps popped on my arms immediately, and for once, I was at a loss for words and could only point my fly rod at them. Sharks everywhere. Besides praying to not let me fall overboard during the fight, I became keenly aware of the adrenaline rush I had wanted and needed.

Suddenly, one of the dorsal fins turned and headed straight for the boat and chum bag. Watching reruns of "Jaws" the night before didn't help the nerves. I readied the rod, and as the fish neared, I lobbed the hunk of feathers, trying to land it just in front of the shark's nose. As it splashed perfectly on the water, the head raised up while a set of teeth, of which there were too many to count, bit down on my fly. A slight pull backward along with the three strong strip sets, and it was on.

I braced my knees against the inside wall of the boat and prepared for the action. The only sound I could hear was the singing of the reel being emptied rather quickly. The captain turned the boat towards the beast as I tried to recover the line. The shark jumped and did an aerial 360. My knees became weak watching the action, but I could not move them. They were stiff and felt superglued to the gel coating. Later, I discovered that I had pressed so hard that my kneecaps had red "strawberries" across the top of them. The goosebumps never left.

Twenty-five minutes into this match, my arms started to ache, and I wished more time had been spent in the gym! As the shark began to tire and I regained line, we finally brought it alongside the boat. My admiration for the fight I just experienced from this sleek and toothy critter is often thought about. The captain lassoed the tail, and we held tight while he very carefully took a long-nosed pair of pliers and dislodged the hook.

Just shy of four feet in length, this first spinner shark, with its sense of determination and ability to rapidly test both the angler and the equipment, is to be admired. This fast, agile predator with its airborne acrobatics is indeed a true gamefish!

We caught several smaller sharks that morning, all black tips and spinners. All were brought into the boat, unhooked, photographed, and released. But nothing compared to the adrenaline rush of that first one!

Redfish Adventure

After spending countless years chasing trout in the mountains, I decided it was time to head towards the coast to chase some redfish. Reading the Internet and trying to soak up all the knowledge prior to my trip, I thought would help me to be successful. Maybe. It was time to experience my own personal DIY (Do It Yourself) saltwater wade fishing adventure.

Fifteen years have passed since my first trial and error in this new saltwater world. Telling stories about those days spent wading salt marshes over a few beers with friends still causes excruciating laughter. I soon learned that I knew a whole lot less than I had thought.

There were too many new variables not understood, which complicated the puzzle of catching redfish in the marsh versus just loading my fly rod, waders, several thousand flies in a vest and taking off to the river.

I remember vividly that first summer chasing redfish. The allure of catching such a tenacious fighter on the fly actually kept me up nights focused solely on this ambition. These new passions never mindfully arrive at the right season, either. I can't remember what triggered this thought process about redfish, probably an article I read somewhere, but I started my exploratory adventure in the dead of winter and soon became consumed. On the bright side, I had five months to plan and learn. On the dark side, my patience was quickly wearing thin.

I recollect my first foray into this salt experience. The 3 ½ hour drive one way made for a long day. I arrived at what I thought to be a productive place in the middle of a vast salt marsh, sat down, and started swatting mosquitoes while waiting for a high tide to show up that never arrived. Somehow, I had miscalculated the tide based on my location and didn't realize a six-foot tide was needed to peak over the high mud banks. This particular tide was only four-feet, therefore never flooding the marsh. The mosquitos won out, and after four hours of sweltering heat and swatting bugs, I walked back to the truck, broken-hearted and smelling like a can of OFF Spray.

In the interim, I studied tide charts and found an afternoon tide that would reach the minimum six-foot requirement, so I started planning again. By this time, I had also tied enough redfish flies to last several folks an entire lifetime.

High tide was supposed to be full about an hour after sundown, which left plenty of daylight to fish before high water and total darkness fell. Again, I arrived a little early and decided I should find the feeder creeks, as the main water channel would probably empty into these first and then drain off. The temperature was a humid 90-plus degrees on the coast of South Carolina, with very little sea breeze. It didn't take but one attempt to learn that tall marsh grass had a soft bottom and to focus my attention on the short grass. That mistake almost cost me a sandal.

Time almost stood still until the water eventually began flowing up the ditches or impressions, just as I had suspected. I tactically decided to position myself above where they shallow out.

Catching a glimpse of that first redfish dorsal fin above the water's surface line almost caused a malady called "Buck Fever." Watching the fish dance on its nose, picking up fiddler crabs in twelve inches of water, with its tail balancing its submerged half, is a vision I will never forget. And the red and yellow hues of a fading sun mirrored in its scales. The black spots encircled by light orange coloring on its tail were like eyes observing my every step. I stalked carefully so as not to make him blink.

My concentration became intently focused on the redfish. Coupled with excitement and months of wrestling with my impatience, it happened. Instead of placing a soft cast three feet in front of the fish, I accurately dropped the fly on its head. I never saw the fish depart, but the wake and marsh mud explosion told me what I needed. My education process was learning the hard way. It wasn't until later that summer, when fishing with Captain John Irwin of FlyRight Charters, I learned to visually focus on the spot ahead. Of course, my hook-up percentages changed drastically with that tidbit of information.

Standing stoic and heron-like, I intently searched for movement again. I could feel the tickle of fiddler crabs inch cautiously across the top of my bare foot. A few minutes later, I looked down and saw a blue crab perched on my foot with claws extended. The pain was so excruciating from trying not to wiggle my toes. I dared not move. Reminded me of how often my nose would itch every time I went for an eye examination. Finally, my new friend wandered off and I could again focus on my intended quarry.

The third shot at a redfish was the charmer! My cast landed in front of the fish, and I slowly twitched it as it approached.

Hookset! Thrashing fish! Gone!

My subconscious trout hook setting techniques, carefully executed through many years of practice, were not strong enough to allow hook penetration into their rock-hard mouths. For a few split seconds, I understood what a redfish adrenaline rush was all about! And then it was gone, and the rush was replaced with agony and disappointment. More determined than ever, my success would soon one day blossom. History repeated itself several times that day.

As the colors of sunset changed to darkness, I just stood knee-deep in the marsh, only me, fish, and a rising tide. With a late arriving moon, stars peeped and glittered brightly with each passing minute. I could feel the push of saltwater moving in, marking the end of high tide. Where did the time go? Enjoying nature has a way of making time eclipse faster than I would prefer.

I was enchanted with the whole experience. I tried to inhale and replay the entire afternoon while I stood there. Several hookups occurred, but nothing was brought to hand. As daylight passed, the amphitheater of stars rotated 180 degrees with no streetlights to dampen their effect. The smell of saltwater and marsh was totally captivating.

My body gauge of the water line now was about thigh deep, and part of me had decided I should wade back to my truck. But the other part of me wasn't quite ready to leave. I was standing alone, absorbing the vastness of the marsh in darkness.

Suddenly, I felt a brush of skin rub against my submerged, bare leg. A stingray, shark, or dolphin, I wondered. Then flashbacks of watching the Discovery Channel, showing great white sharks tossing seals high in the air, convinced me I needed to hastily wade back out of the dark water. The faint outline of my white truck sitting high on a sandy road pointed me in the right direction. My legs moved like a propeller on a flats boat at full throttle, headed home. The once empty marsh bottom was now a salt pond brimming with swimming creatures looking for a meal.

With my creative imagination, the size of whatever rubbed against my leg will never be known, but the speed at which I departed concluded an evening that will never be forgotten.

On a warm summer's day, standing still in the marsh looking for blades of grass to part, a dorsal fin to show, grasping the thought of hooking just one tailing redfish will forever bring goosebumps.

Stripers in the Capital City

Have you ever paused for a moment and thought about what the rest of the world is doing at that precise time? This fleeting thought happened to me not long ago as the aluminum-reinforced jet-driven Jon boat scooted the currents, rocks, and rapids of the Saluda River, passing underneath two interstates near downtown Columbia, South Carolina.

Walking down the boat ramp at daylight in late spring, I could feel the chill that cold rivers give in early mornings. This tailwater is released below dams and is cold. Like mountain streams in sunlight, the air here in the Piedmont region had the same chilly feeling as I climbed into the boat. It could be a hint of excitement and anticipation coupled with a slight breeze as it blew its breath of freshness downriver. Jackets are required at dawn.

As the sun's first rays appeared, the automatic lights flickered off from the tall buildings that outlined this capital city's backdrop. Above me were exhaust fumes, red taillights, horns, police sirens, and a traffic jam that permeated the morning solitude on the congested interstate. Looking below this mighty bridge, I noticed several deer fording the river and congregating on dry land at the base of a pilon holding I-126 steady, probably wondering what to do or where to go next. I decided rather quickly not to worry about what the rest of the world was doing because my day job was fly fishing for stripers. Despite all the noise from above, the only sound I could clearly distinguish was the voice of a fish calling my name.

There is a unique striper fishery on the outskirts of Columbia and meandering downstream along the border of downtown. I was here to test the waters. Several sets of rapids, caused by hydroelectric generation of dams upstream, created challenges to navigate the boat. White water, dynamic currents, and boulders made the ride interesting. Careful not to spill my coffee, I sat back and, for once, I was glad that I wasn't driving the boat.

I was with Justin McGrady, a long-time resident, guide, and die-hard striper fisherman who intimately knew the river and its different moods. A lifetime spent on the river enabled him to maneuver the boat easily through the maze of boulders and rapids in search of fish. Local knowledge is always a good companion to have on any new adventure. While moving through aerated rapids to new locations, we passed kayakers enjoying the foamy ride down.

Patches of fog, not yet burned off by the sun, hovered over pockets of flat eddies, giving the Saluda a mysterious mood. Spanish moss lay draped across the arms of many trees, fooling me into thinking I was closer to the coast than I actually was. Water lilies were still blooming. Their white blooms dotted the river corridor and added a classic touch of elegance to where the Broad and the

Saluda Rivers converged to form the Congaree. This river empties into the Santee Reservoir lakes and eventually the ocean near Charleston, South Carolina.

In the spring, stripers run out of the lower lakes and head north to spawn, putting them into this river chain. I had never seen the entire Saluda from the confluence of these rivers back to Lake Murray Dam and was excited to meet these river nomads firsthand. I have always thought river fish were more powerful than their lake cousins, and I wanted to test my theory. In tandem with the powerful fish surges when hooked, one must fight the strength of river currents, and fish know how to use them to their advantage.

Between Justin and me, we had an arsenal of nine-weight and ten-weight fly rods with sinking lines, sink tip lines, and a floating line. I never had enough confidence to take only ten shells to a dove shoot, and I feel the same way about flies. Preferring the philosophical approach of "more is better," my fly box is stuffed full of four- to eight-inch streamers, hooks sharpened and ready for action.

Large popping bugs were thrown early into pockets and eddies with no luck. Very little surface activity was seen. We switched over to sinking lines with long, white and chartreuse articulated streamers with large eyes. Casting into foam lines and drifting downstream initiated a flurry of activity.

The sinking lines allowed the large articulated flies to get down to the fish much quicker in the swift currents. Casting across and then mending upstream quickly allowed the fly to swing downstream. The fishing was slow early, and with adrenaline flowing, the stripping action of the fly was probably too fast. We had several large fish estimated to be 35- to 40-inches each follow the fly back to the boat, only to have them spook when they saw us. Seeing these fish only enhanced the impatient "fish rush" of hooking one, and my knees wanted to buckle.

I could relax once the first striper was hooked, fought, and released. The striper was a nice 5 lb. fish that knew how to grab the downstream currents and pull drag brutally. Stripers don't tail dance on the water's surface like largemouth bass. Instead, they use bulldog strength to dive for rocks, boulders, crevices, and cover. This causes the fly rod to bend halfway down while my imagination fabricates images of unusually large fish on the end. After all these years, I have learned not to be disappointed if the fish doesn't meet my imaginative size expectations after the fight.

I find it always interesting that most fish caught are compared to the first, and this trip was no different. Comments like, "The first one was a lot bigger," or "The first one fought harder." "Look closely at how fat this fish is; it didn't swallow the fly like the first one. Maybe it just instinctively swiped?" Other comparisons include, "The fish are getting smaller! What are we doing wrong?"

"I wish we had about five or six the size of that first one!" And finally, "This is twice the size of the first one -let's keep casting!"

 It's never about the sheer number of fish caught, but the experience of feeling the pressure placed against carbon fiber rolled like a pencil and bending. And the fly reel, buzzing and yielding fly line with every pull and surge. Then you finally get to see all the fuss as the fish nears the boat, only to be spooked and then run away for one more escape attempt. My fish adrenaline rush never left me all day.

On this overcast and humid day, we caught and released seven nice stripers. With the currents running south, each fish felt bigger as they darted downstream at the first sign of a hook set. Then it would cut across the river seams and head for the safety of large boulders tucked into the back eddies of each current.

As a prelude to any fishing trip, the night before yields little sleep but rather dreams of massive fish that succumb to my fly. I always seem to wake up before any are ever landed and can't figure that part out. Like most fishing trips, the biggest fish merely followed our flies back to the boat without tasting how delicious fur and feathers can be. But the ones we did catch were fun. I never hooked a fish I didn't like.

During the trip back downriver and heading to the landing, I looked behind me and once again saw the snarled mess and traffic jam of a congested interstate filled with folks trying to get home. The evening lights of the big city could be seen lighting up against a darkening sky. Tomorrow, I will again visit the rest of the world and all the craziness, but for now, I go home fulfilled, tired and at peace.

Ones That Got Away, A Few That Didn't

"Smoked carp tastes just as good as smoked salmon when you ain't got no smoked salmon."
~ Patrick F. McManus

Missing Excuses

Fly fishing, like all types of fishing, can be full of "misses." And with every "miss," there is usually a barrage of excuses that help explain such occurrences.

If we stay outdoors enough, we soon discover that "missing" can be a natural occurrence. Some examples of my life's near misses include both hunting and fly fishing experiences. To me, they all seem to run together.

One hot September Saturday afternoon, I expired 16 straight rounds of high-powered #8 shot and nary dusted a dove's tail feather. My poor Lab looked at me with an exasperated and disgusted look after each consecutive "missed" shot, and I felt ashamed for both of us. I reasoned that I probably needed a new shotgun, along with booking an appointment with my ophthalmologist.

Several years ago, I "missed" a nice trophy buck. If that deer had been a tad closer, stood broadside, and not walked away from me, and if I had practiced my breathing instead of panting before I pulled the trigger, which, by the way, should have been adjusted to a lighter setting, I would have scored. Realistically, I probably got a severe dose of buck fever and "missed" the shot.

Many years ago, we were cruising the swamps of Lake Marion in lower South Carolina and had successfully caught bream and a few bass on popping bugs throwing them near the base of cypress trees. Finally, it was time to leave, as the darkness would be upon us soon, and this was the last place I wanted to be after dark. After an hour of cruising around the swamp, I looked at my buddy and confessed I must have "missed" a couple of the important landmarks and humbly confessed we were lost.

I used the word "missing" a lot as a verb, trying to explain and justify to my wife why I had just charged a new fly rod on our credit card. I tried to compare the action of this new rod I had cast at the fly shop to a rod I sold 15 years ago and had really "missed." The flex on this new rod was similar and smooth, and I really had been attached to that old rod and fought depression for weeks after selling it. The plan almost worked, except that she noticed the separate fly reel purchase on the statement weeks later.

Being primarily a "die-hard" fly fisherman, I have discovered that "missing" a fish is a part of life, and have learned to accept it. That doesn't mean I always have to like it, but the fact is, it's an integral part of fishing.

Over the years, I have tried to develop a standardized mental Dewey Decimal System catalog of excuses when I "miss" a fish. I revert to it regularly.

I remember casting to an extremely large rainbow feeding on top (I can't quantify his size because I didn't catch it), but seeing the wake and rings he left after rising brought chill bumps.
I waded quietly to where I could place myself in the correct position to allow the fly to land feet above him, careful to cast only once and not line him. This would allow the fly to land softly, then gently ride the currents down. I carefully watched as he continued to feed. Like music, I felt a connection to this fish and could understand his rhythm of rising and feeding.

Finally, it was time. A perfect cast, the fly drifted slowly into his feeding lane and his body gently rose, breaking the surface first with his head and then his dorsal fin. He was huge, and I was enamored with the sight. As he tilted up and opened his mouth to inhale my dainty little yellow fly and submerge, I lifted the rod up and could feel his strength pull back, the surge and power of a large fish. I was confident he was mine.

I instantaneously began thinking about all the pics of this monster I could send back to my buddies during these brief split seconds of action. And then it was over. My fish saliva-slimed fly floated downstream as my leader straightened out, and I stood there in cold thigh-deep water. Broken-hearted, fishless, as my mind headed down the fish "missing" trail of thoughts about which excuse and reason I could use for this miss.

Lucky for me, I had a plethora of them.

Using barbless hooks, I accidentally gave it slack, and the hook dislodged during the hook set.

I am sure I just lifted the rod tip too high when setting the hook and did not perform a big fish "hook set."

When I lifted and pulled the rod tip up, my tippet stretched excessively out of proportion.

The fly floatant made the fly too slick and it just slid out the fish's mouth.

Maybe I had hung an unseen underwater snag, and it really wasn't that fish I had almost caught after all.

The rocky river bottom is somewhat slick and I may have accidentally and unknowingly slipped backward without realizing it during all the fish-hooking commotion. Next time, I'll wear my wading shoes with a cleated bottom for more foot-gripping action instead of just plain felt.

I should have checked the fly more carefully beforehand when I got hung in the rhododendron and had to climb up the bank to dislodge it. Or when I hooked the lower limb of a sycamore tree or caught a piece of bark off an old water-soaked log behind me, not to mention the wet leaves the fly dragged underwater while I crossed over a small rock dam.

Depressing as it may sound, in its haste to catch a meal, maybe the fish just "missed" my fly outright, and I happened to snag the body instead. I would never repeat this excuse out loud.

But there is always a silver lining. I still had my fly. It was a perfectly proportioned upright winged fly tied 35 years ago when my eyesight was much better. I had kept it in the fly box with several others like it for good luck all these years. Although it may have gotten damp a few times, there wasn't much rust on the hook point when I tied it on.

"Missing" a nice fish does lend itself to bragging rights. I can proudly boast about the large fish I "almost caught" while my buddies steadily hooked smaller ones.

Being a repeat "missed" offender on fish, one of these days, I will man up and say, "I missed it," with absolutely no excuse. Either way, I'll keep fishing and practicing my "misses." And maybe I will write a story about my "saltwater miss" excuses one day, too.

My Ghost Fish

Has there ever been a fish that you have hooked and lost, which has haunted you? Maybe it's a fish still hidden beneath a dock, under a log, or tucked into some other invisible concealment. The thought of this lost fish just floats in memory, constantly replaying every detail of your encounter.

If a person fishes long enough, there too will be a ghost fish in their lifetime. I have one that haunted me. It was a big rainbow of many seasons that, without exaggeration, could easily be a trout of a lifetime. What really becomes more disturbing to me is the fact that I had hooked this "ghost fish" on more than one occasion, and through fish karma, it continues to elude me.

Remembering important details clutters my thoughts, and the different hookups merge into one. Details run together, including trip planning and preparation, air temperature, and forecast down to the barometric pressure, water level, and clarity, what time of day I hooked the fish, and why I chose a particular fly! Was my tippet material too small? Was the fly tied on the wrong kind of hook and not strong enough? Maybe I used the wrong kind of knot and didn't cinch it down tight and double-check it.

I can vividly see its lair and know intimately the small run, coupled with pocket water, it calls home. The undercut bank provides refuge from predators peering from above. There are three large rocks above this pocket of water that break the current and create a back eddy. The eddy is deep, and the bottom, flushed out from seasons of high water and sudden storms, now contains primarily pea gravel. A white, bubbly, foam line runs around the rocks and affords the opportunistic fish a quick meal and safely returns home. Past experience tells me the undercut bank is a tippet magnet that has become a forest of roots, providing a secure maze through which only a fish can manipulate.

It's a difficult section to get a true drag-free float with a nymph and/or a dry fly. The tricky currents require high sticking of the fly rod. Fishing the edge of the white foam where the stream flows beside the rocks consistently produces some smaller rainbows. Knowing that "Moby Dick" lurks inside the foam line next to the bank makes putting steel to fish lips of the smaller rainbows appear as only practice. Though I really like to catch fish of all sizes, the thought of that monster peering skywards through the mirrored water at my futile attempts to fool him is frustrating.

This section of the river is open to the public, and I worry that somebody will catch my fish before I finally get a chance to land him. I want to admire his olive back, the vibrant red stripe that runs the length of his body, and the silvery underside, which blends into a pearl iridescent color as it nears the tail. He would be gently unhooked and released back into the current to find respite inside the undercut bank. I just yearn for another chance.

I have hooked him on several occasions, and the fight lasted just a brief second each time. Either a knot broke, or the fly popped out, showing a poor hookset. Adrenaline, coupled with excitement, divided by frustration, multiplied by rapid heartbeats, seemingly took place quickly. And I was left standing in knee-deep water empty-handed, holding onto a memory of an apparition that instinctively disappeared.

I recollect an early spring overcast afternoon when I had the river to myself. It was unusual. Not another car in the parking lot or footprints ahead of me along the river's bank. A true afternoon of solitude, the sounds of a running river, the cold water running through my legs, and the aromatic invigoration of fresh air.

I stopped and fished a few small runs and managed to hook and release several small fish, but my sights were focused on the big rainbow. Was he still there?

Midges and small blue-winged olive mayflies were hatching and bouncing off the water's surface. They became more prolific as the afternoon passed and I hiked up the path on the river's edge. Several fish began breaking the surface and inhaling the adult insects as they rode the current, drying their wings. On any other day, I would have stopped to enjoy fishing a dry fly as the insects were hatching like popcorn everywhere, surrounded by receptive and hungry fish.

Would today be the time when I finally get to hook up and really see this "ghost fish" that had taken up permanent residence in my head? I eased around the river bend and stood next to the hemlock, attempting to conceal myself, and just watched. As I had thought, the smaller rainbows fed feverishly in the foamy current. I sat and enjoyed the show, looking for my one particular fish.

On the corner of a rock, careful not to distance himself from the undercut bank, he began to feed. Slowly, his head would break the surface and just inhale an insect. Again and again, he fed. I became mesmerized by this enormous fish sipping such a tiny mayfly so delicately that I dared not move to disturb him.

It was then I felt a connection. A wild fish survives. Prior details of hooking and losing him became clear but were no longer so important. I had no expectations of him being there that day but hoped he would. Now that I knew he was there, as I watched him feed secretly, I just sat there with focused admiration.

The insect hatch slowed almost as quickly as it had begun, and he mysteriously disappeared back into the undercut bank. I got up and fished my way back towards the truck, casting dry flies and catching stragglers still hungry.

I had seen my "ghost fish" and felt a pensive realm of calmness while memories of previous frustrations vanished. I left the river that night in a satisfied and excited mood; I had come to grips with my "ghost fish."

The Day the River Exploded

Every fly fishing trip is an adventure and, ultimately, a story to be retold later with some degree of accuracy. Likewise, I have always viewed every trip as a success as well, regardless of the outcome. Optimism is part of my nature and makes the story more interesting.

Despite all the various obstacles thrown at me during fishing trips, such as leaky waders, felt soles falling off a pair of worn-out wading shoes or the laces popping from dry rot, high water, falling in or stepping over my head, having the right fly rod but the wrong reel spooled with the wrong line, not catching a fish because I don't have the right fly or should have been there yesterday, and, lest we forget, the weather, which is always ready to "enliven" the experience.

During the last 50 years, I have learned not to fully trust weather forecasters, even though the weather does play an important role in success. Forecasters are probably the only folks that can consistently lie and get away with it. Inconsistent weather patterns make it hard to plan a fishing trip, especially if any substantial travel is involved. But once planned, it's best to just go anyway, despite the weather. Therefore, I always pack what I think I need, pack some extra, and then go fishing. It makes for a less stressful event but with a much heavier gear bag.

Not long ago, I was invited by an old friend to fish a new section of a particular river I had not fished before. New rivers and new sections of old rivers help perpetuate stories. I peered at my iPhone to check the weather before leaving home. I was confident I had packed all the necessities, and the weather forecast showed only brief showers around noon and then clearing up. Perfect fishing weather, I thought. A great day to fish, with overcast skies and a light sprinkle to break up the water's surface.

Turning off the paved road, I proceeded down a muddy, dirt logging track to the put-in. Standing water with excessively deep mud puddles was evidence that the forecast was again wrong.

Despite another wrong forecast, we were determined to fish. We picked up our gear and walked a hundred yards in the rain over to a dry place to get ready. Sometimes fly fishermen, in their haste to suit up, do unexplainable things.

Stringing a fly rod has a calming effect and helps to start focusing on the task at hand, much like an anxiety pill-taking effect. This formality brings a heightened concentration level and occurs to some degree in all sports. I've watched football players slap each other on the helmet and then bang their heads together. That doesn't work for fly fishing. Assembling a fly rod and reel at the riverbank is a ritual that helps perpetuate anticipation of wading a new river and thoughts of big fish to hook.

The rain ceased momentarily as we walked upstream, looking for the perfect spot to enter the river. Its clarity was questionable, but we were there to fish, so we began. I rigged up my favorite fly, a heavy woolly bugger with rubber legs tied kind of squirmy, affectionately called "The Attitude." The name defines my imitation and persona when I tie this fly on. Deciding to add a small dropper fly would hopefully increase my hook rate, not to include doubling my fly loss when I got tangled in the bushes. With the higher-colored water, I thought it to be the perfect combination. The only thing missing was a fish with an open mouth.

It's always a pleasure to fish in new water, see new places, and accidentally learn a few new tricks from the fish. How amazing that a small-brained creature can humble a person wearing so much fishing gear. If only they understood how much all this cost. For the first hour, I fished the foam edges and pockets created by boulders pushing and funneling water in turmoil downstream.

A strike here, then hooking a small one until he wrestled off the barbless hook, kept things interesting. All rivers have their own personality, and it was exciting to introduce myself to this one. Overhanging laurels and rhododendrons dipping in the water's edge and moss-covered rocks outcropping above the surface looked inviting areas to cast, too. The bottom was a good mixture of flat stones and sand pockets, which made it easy to wade along the edge.

The rain kept steadily pouring down. The river rose gently and became slightly discolored. My buddy's jacket was soaking up the moisture rather than reflecting it. For some reason, I had tucked my raincoat inside my waders versus keeping it on the outside, thus creating a water slide allowing rain inside of my wader legs. Goretex waders and jacket did their job by keeping the river out and rainwater in. Despite the minor discomforts, we kept fishing. Feeding fish always takes priority.

As we continued working our way down the river, casting into pockets and fishing foam line tailouts, trying to keep the nymphs bouncing on the bottom, I looked downriver to see my buddy's fly line go tight and the rod arc. He nodded confidently, which is a form of nonverbal communication to other fly fishermen that a good fish is hooked. I watched him play the fish with confidence and offered to net it. A nice rainbow was scooped up, fist bumps, pictures and then released. Pouring rain was becoming a minor inconvenience.

With the steady rain, the river became more discolored and increased in volume and the fish kept biting. The coffee-colored water made wading both good and bad. We had to feel the bottom more with our boots while maneuvering around rocks, but the fish weren't as spooky with that extra layer of discolored protection.

I changed the dropper fly and went down to a small size 18 nymph tied with a hint of flash and ultraviolet dubbing material. There was an eddy that looked deep and inviting and calling to that fly. As the river tumbled across several large rocks, it created a back channel where the fast water had carved a pocket.

To sink the fly deep, I cast above the rocks and let the water guide my fly deep into the eddy. As it cleared rapids, I felt a bump or a strike and set the hook. Nothing happened. Did I just set the hook into a snag? Maybe, but the snag felt heavy. As I applied pressure, the snag began to carefully and steadily move up and down in the current. More subtle pressure from the rod tip and I quickly realized the rather large, heavy swimming snag had fins. It was slowly wavering to the left and then deep again. Whatever was swimming below my rod tip was in charge and I knew it. Hopefully, I could gain control when it decided to test my nerves, knots and tackle.

And then it happened. Maybe the fish realized it wasn't in total control or was tired of not maneuvering where it wanted to go. Either way, the water exploded like a grenade had been dropped, sending tsunami waves into the bank of this small stream.

A huge rainbow materialized above the surface. Its body was too big to get airborne fully. It started frantically crashing the water's surface, pulling at the tip of my rod and pulling out the fly line. The beauty, strength and size of this fish were humbling. I have caught and lost big fish, but this fish was different. Naturally, my thought process was overcome with concern for anything that could go wrong. I needed to keep thinking positively and live in the moment. Would my knots hold? Surely, a mental defeat and solemn drive home would follow if this fish was lost due to a poorly tied knot.

The fish violently erupted, displacing a rather large volume of water with its return to its liquid home. The fish even sounded heavy, with a deep thud like a large rock being dumped into a pond. Several surface bursts later, it began to thrust itself into the rapids, trying to escape. And then, after a couple more acrobatic leaps, I realized quickly a new strategy was needed. During the last airborne display, I noticed the small blackish-purple fly was hooked in the upper right corner of the mouth, and a tug from the wrong direction would pull the fly out.

Scrambling to climb up the bank, I swiftly headed downstream to get better leverage on this behemoth. The river was probably thirty feet wide with a deep run in the middle, and my goal was to hold the fish upstream with positive pressure to keep the fly lodged in place. When it did try to run downstream, I jumped and thrashed myself, spooking the rainbow back upriver. Keeping tight leverage was my only hope of landing it.

My buddy waded into my right side, and after four attempts, my prize was finally secured in his net. The struggle had taken twelve minutes of maneuvering and feeling my heart beating, pounding the inside of my rain jacket like a hammer on a nail. I felt as worn out as the fish but had accomplished my mission. I stood there, reflecting on the battle.

Until I heard the bellowing words, "My net is tearing!"

With a bearhug wrap, he attempted to hold the fish against his chest while I ran back upstream to get my big net. Too big to grab and pull out, I eased down in the shallows and lifted this monster into my large net while trying to revive the fish and myself simultaneously.

As with every fish, there needs to be a sense of humility and thankfulness for the opportunity to be standing in cold, clean water and fishing. This fish provided wonderful memories that will last my lifetime and probably be spun into various stories wrapped in extreme truths.

As I gently held this river monster headfirst into the current, I could watch its gills pump oxygen as it swayed back and forth in my hands. Its tail garnered momentum and strength as it eased itself back into the current, heading towards that corner eddy. I watched the fish swim away with respect and admiration and felt humbled to have even witnessed the event. Tired, rain-soaked and wet, I looked at my buddy and asked, "Where's the next run?"

Boys, Ponds, and Big Creatures

Ponds full of largemouth, crappie, and bream, along with other mysterious critters, are special places. Whether fishing from an old Jon boat, paddling and sneaking around the edges, or just standing on the bank, each time I fish a pond, I have recollections of days gone by as a youngster. Compared to a large reservoir, the success rate for catching fish on a farm pond has always been higher for me.

In my early years, I can remember Dad going into a cane patch near the house and cutting the longest and straightest cane poles he could find. Then, he would tie each by its tip from a high tree limb, add a brick for weight, and let them dangle and dry. After 3 to 4 weeks, he would varnish them and add some line, a hook, a split shot and a cork. With a cup full of worms, we had dug up around his flower beds, through the woods and off to the pond above the house we would go.

He once told me that I needed to start a worm farm to support my fondness for pond fishing. So, after returning from a successful pond trip, I counted and emptied the remaining 17 worms into a shady wooded area. Then, I rearranged some mulch from a flower bed and poured a bag of dry grits and coffee grounds on it daily for two weeks. It was a responsible job for a seven-year-old.

After such time had passed, I dug up worms for an inventory and found only 16 wigglers and no babies. Evidently, my worm farm wasn't much of a success. But the fishing continued, and with it, a passion that would evolve into a lifetime pursuit.

After my first year in college, I took one trip to a mountain stream to try my hand at fly fishing for trout. Afterward, all I could think about was fly fishing. An obsession was born. And from that grew another passion: fly tying. Forty-seven years later, I've never regretted these addictions. Chests-of-drawers stuffed with hooks, fur, feathers, and an array of Tupperware boxes full of miscellaneous materials now decorate the "man room."

Every time I see a small body of water, call it a pond, lake, or swamp, I can't help but think about my beginning days with a cane pole. Instead of a cup of wigglers, I have replaced them with emptied Altoid boxes loaded with homemade popping bugs, nymphs, and streamers. Ponds offer me a simpler life and a nice change of pace from waders, multiple fly boxes, and navigating mountain streams.

Recently, heavy rains forced the creeks and mountain streams I usually haunt to be too high for wading and totally unfishable. I really needed to scratch the fish itch. Fortunately, I prescribed a trip to a farm pond with a friend to remedy this malady.

I noticed an old-standing cane patch next to the shed as we unloaded the 14-foot Jon boat. A quick trip down memory lane ensued. The excitement of a new pond adventure has never left this old man.

Being late February, with the water still chilly, I decided to throw a 10-foot sink-tip fly line with small streamers. Hearing rumors of multiple brush piles in this particular pond, I crammed additional flies in both Altoid boxes, making them hard to shut.

This went against my nature, as I believe ponds reflect a simpler fly fishing style and shouldn't require all the necessities of stream fishing. But I do break my own rules now and then.

We launched the little boat and began working, likely looking for "fishy" spots. Several casts later, there was a hookup to a nice bass. Expectations and the actual truth about the results don't always match up, but the stories usually exceed expectations. Looking at the middle of the pond, we tried to imagine the creek channel, then fish it down to the spillway. Casting off to deeper water yielded good results and kept the bass action going.

A large brush pile a couple hundred yards away appeared irresistible to fish. We paddled over and began bombing flies around the stickups. A couple of small basses tasted some fur and feathers, and then it happened.

At first, I thought it was a log, and another fly lost. Then it moved slightly to the right and down. Whatever was on the other end of my fly line was big and heavy. The log started pulling our little Jon boat across the pond, and I wondered if a big catfish had swallowed my fly. Surely, a trophy bass would have jumped several times and acted crazy. Thoughts of an extremely large fish embraced my inner being, and the longer it fought, the more intense the thoughts.

Then, it got tired and began to surface slowly. My fly rod was entirely bent in half, and I expected it to snap. But I kept swapping it from the left to the right, trying to angle against candy-caning the tip. Had I worn this unknown catch out? I saw it like a nuclear sub surfacing after several months of a secret mission. Bubbles first, then a large round shell broke the surface with colossal-sized legs violently clawing through the water. Its head reared up, looking me in the eye with disgust and madness, appearing very inconvenienced.

There was my streamer, hooked in the upper right leg. Did I strip-set the fly too fast and miss its mouth, or was it just a clean snag? I spoke more of the first option and briefly bragged to my friend that all creatures find my flies appetizing. Now all I wanted was my fly back, and I was determined to get it. But a plan was needed.

I reached over to grab its tail in order to flip the snapper for a better angle. Using needle nose pliers, I was ready to snatch out my fly. That particular streamer had been successful today, and I only had one more like it, so its return was important.

As I reached down, I noticed the snapping turtle's head popped out much farther than expected, with jaws that gapped open almost four inches. I jumped back, rocking the little boat sideways. A quick management decision was made to let him wear this new piece of jewelry until the hook rusted out. I wondered if I could ever land this behemoth on a cane pole.

Taking a breather from the excitement, I noticed a muskrat swimming along the shore while a pair of wood ducks circled and landed in a creek channel behind us. It was great just to be outside, and all the catching made it perfect. Several crappies later and a few small basses caught to keep it interesting, dusk set in and topped the afternoon off.

It doesn't matter how many streams I wade, mountains I climb, or new areas I explore; there will always be something special about pond fishing that brings out the little boy in me.

Now, where did I put those worms?

Of Flies and Rods

"Every fly fishing trip is an adventure and, ultimately, a story to be retold later with some degree of accuracy." ~ the Author

As My Fly Rod Slowly Snaps…

Did you ever own that perfect pair of leather boots that actually fit the first time you tried them on? They didn't hurt when they broke in. They were waterproof and somewhat warm but not overly hot on those long mountain hikes. These boots made each step comfortable and didn't tear up after a yearlong sloshing in puddles, and they climbed over rocks well--they were just a joy to slide your foot in. Wearing them signified an adventure was beginning to unfold. With all the boots and shoes a person might own, there is always one pair that, no matter how worn and ratty they might look, you can't get yourself to throw out.

There's little difference between an old pair of comfortable boots and a fly rod. Each rod serves a particular purpose in different situations. A person can't have too many fly rods. There may be a rod for low summertime streams, small brookie streams, tailraces, panfish, bass bugs, streamer fishing, and saltwater. I have tried to explain this concept to my wife, and I think it finally hit home when I compared my fly rods to her shoe closet.

With a closet full of fly rods from which to choose, I always gravitate back to one in particular. Everyone has their favorite. During the winter, I may inventory all my rods, take them out of the case, put them together, and wiggle the tip beneath the "man room" ceiling fan. Swinging the rod rapidly back and forth doesn't tell me a lot about the action, but it does remind me how it feels with cork in hand. With each different rod, I reminisce about the fishing trips taken, the fish caught, and the laughs all my friends and I shared on the outings. Then I stow the memories and the rod back into the aluminum tube, pick up another, and smile.

Like that old, worn pair of boots, I feel the same about a specific fly rod. There is one nine foot, five-weight rod that I consistently grab when it's time to chase trout. I don't understand the emotional attachment to this inanimate object, but there is one. As I recall, I paid full price for it in the fly shop many years ago. But I've never regretted the investment. The casting stroke seems magical and methodical with it in hand. The way it plays fish, bending between the fourth and fifth line guides, helps to feel each fish's vibration, pull, and surge. I think about fishing some of the other rods and sometimes do, but in the back of my mind, my subconscious tells me I should have grabbed the "other one." And that's OK.

This rod has traveled the country for more than two decades and hooked fish in numerous states. Evidence of our adventures can be seen on the rod tube, almost destroyed from being thrown in the back of pickups, rolled around on floorboards, stepped on, shoved into airplane storage bins, and various other waves of abuse. But that's the tube's purpose: to serve and protect.

When I bought the fly rod, it was considered a "fast action" rod, and if someone different cast it now, they would probably consider it a medium action rod. I don't get caught up in all that hype anymore. It fits me and my casting style. I sometimes wonder if the rod just actually fit my casting style or if I changed my style to fit the rod. Either way, it works.

After all the years and all the trips, disaster finally struck. I broke THE rod. I have always been careful about an errant cast causing my fly to connect with bushes, mountain laurels, tree limbs, and grass and then pulling back hard to extract the fly. When wade fishing, I may fish for a long period of time before the inevitable happens. My fly got hung up and hung up again and again until the "hung up" spell was either broken or my tippet snapped.

It wasn't a snag that caused its temporary demise but a miscalculation of my wading boot meant to land firmly and solid on a rock below the water's surface. Somehow, since my last trip there, a tree root grew quickly out of nowhere and managed to ensnarl the boot, thus causing me to make a really big splash. I gasped and floundered as the cold water seeped inside my waders.

February water temperatures in the Blue Ridge Mountains can get somewhat chilly. During this quick rush of water, I slapped and kicked all the limbs and branches around me, searching for solid ground as I floated through the pool I had previously wanted to fish. I managed to survive, but my rod, unfortunately, didn't.

I hiked back to the truck to change clothes, grabbed a spare rod from the truck, and proceeded back down to the river to fish. No submerged fall was going to wreck the day I had planned. With each fish caught thereafter, which weren't many, I thought more about my broken rod and our journeys together. The laughs, the adventures with friends, the stories, and the people we've met along the way. Looking down the broken blank were battle scars, small notches where tiny split shots nicked the once smooth finish.

I talked with the manufacturer, who agreed to examine the rod and even offered to replace it with a newer model. I thought about accepting the offer. A new sleek, shiny blank with a faster action than my old one ..but I couldn't replace it. Hopeful of the results, I sent my broken rod back for inspection.

Sitting by the fire on this New Year's Day, I checked my computer and received an email that the old rod was fitted and fixed and will be shipped the first week of January. I was lucky. I was ecstatic. What a great way to start the new year.

My memory drifts back, and I think about the rod, where I have been, my friends all these years who are still here, ready for another adventure, and those who are now up on a heavenly stream, catching fish on every cast, no matter how ugly the fly or sloppy their cast. I still wish they could have been repaired and returned like my old rod, ready to go again.

Of Flies & Fisherman Gone By

During a lifetime spent wading rivers chasing browns, brookies, and rainbows, it seems that memories and details of trips fade like the passing of another day. Trying to remember specifics of older trips in years gone by has eroded.

As time continues its journey, I find that many old fly patterns, once successful, are replaced with newer synthetic materials and newer versions of older flies with different names. I am guilty of this and, like my fishing buddies, always searching for that "secret, never-failing" fly that works 90 percent of the time and is easy to tie. It seems that age is calling for simpler patterns to tie. As with life itself, I need a fly with a lot less complications.

After spending a rainy day rummaging through a chest of drawers full of "stuff" in my fly-tying room, I discovered, hidden under bags of decaying materials, six or seven forgotten fly boxes crammed with "secret flies" from the 1970s, '80s and '90s. My original goal was to provide some type of organization to this chest of stuff, but after finding these flies, my organizational skills came to a halt.

As I held these flies in the palm of my hand, fishing trips transcribed somewhere in a hidden closet of my mind were unlocked. Holding up an old, rusty, size 12 Grey Fox Variant sent me on a float trip back decades ago. Dry fly fishing pocket water and eddies with the fly and catching enough fish to keep it interesting. Where had these memories been?

That was such a great dry fly to fish throughout the Southern Appalachians in late March and April. From fishing foam lines to dabbling in pocket water, the fly regularly produced fish. The late Art Flick promoted this fly, in larger sizes, to be fished during the Green Drake hatches of the Delaware and other upper New York rivers. This fly has consistently been a great searching pattern and has taken fish when no mayfly activity was seen. The striped quill body, combined with an olive thread underbody, gives this fly a segmented effect. Coupled with oversize hackles, it floats extremely well. For reasons unknown, for more than 30 years, this and other flies laid dormant and overlooked in my fly box, hidden in the bottom of a drawer and my memory.

Surprisingly, besides the Grey Fox Variant flies, somewhat mashed down and compressed from other flies, lay several Adams Variants. This particular fly had been my go-to summer pattern in periods of low water during the warmer months. With a golden pheasant tippet tail, yellow ostrich herl body, and grizzly-tipped wings in smaller sizes, it daintily lit upon the water's surface with barely a ripple. Thoughts of early summer mornings on the Davidson River many wild rainbows had difficulty refusing this fly in sizes 16 and 18 when presented properly.

Instead of organizing, I continued to rummage and plunder, searching for other forgotten treasures. And there it was, lying neatly in the back of the bottom drawer, totally obscured from view, was my Fishing Log Notebook dating from the 1970s and 80s. Excitedly flipping pages, I began to read all the journal entries.

Though I may not have been consistently up to date at the time with all my entries, looking back, I marveled how I could retrace my many footsteps. What a personal and wonderful historical find. The notes, shorthand, and scribbling wouldn't mean much to anyone without some type of verbal explanation. I took the wrinkled notebook and sat down in the chair near my tying bench and began to reminisce as I read and deciphered my ridiculously terrible handwriting on those old yellow pages.

"Wednesday, November 20th, 1985. Fishing alone today. The day before Thanksgiving and had taken off to fish the Chattooga River. No cars in the parking lot. It was overcast with highs in the upper 40s and cloudy, and the water temperature was 44 degrees Fahrenheit. Fished towards Reed Creek very stealthy; the water was low and clear. Blue Winged Olives were hatching in several runs, size 20-22, and fished dry to rising fish using parachutes and enjoyed the afternoon. Catching two to three fish per run and then moving up. I felt blessed and thankful to be there."

"Friday, May 2, 1989. Fishing alone on the Davidson River above Avery Creek in the evening. Decided to fish my favorite runs until dark. I sat on the riverbank and ate supper; I needed time to unwind from a hectic week at work. 7:00 P.M. sparse hatches of Light Cahills and Yellow Sallies. Decided to watch for a little while. The Cahills were size 16, light cream in nature. I decided to use a light quill-bodied parachute tied with wood duck wings. The last hour before dark was incredible and filled with 12" wild and frenzied jumping rainbows, which put a good bend in my four-weight rod. I may revisit tomorrow evening!" I didn't document fishing the next evening, but there is a good chance I probably did go.

"June 2nd, 2001, George and I fished the South Holston River below the weir. The sulfurs were very sparse but a few risers. Fished a cranefly pattern with much success and pheasant tail dropper size 18. Mike Harvell, one of my lifelong fishing buddies, had presented me with a ten-foot, five-weight Kennedy Fisher rod, like the one I had bought in 1981 and broken. I nicknamed this rod the "Spirit Rod" in honor of his late father, who had fished it for years. It was previously his rod and had successfully fooled countless fish. What a special gift and every fish caught was a tribute to the previous owner."

The rest of the afternoon was spent on a quiet stroll down memory lane. Any organizational endeavors were forfeited for this hike to the past.

I wouldn't think to write in my fishing journal now after so many trips have passed and years elapsed. Spending a few hours reminiscing and re-living encounters of past fish, fishing trips, and the good times shared with friends is enough for one tattered old log.

Old Fly

My fly boxes are a wreck most of the time. A garbled wad of fur, feathers, and steel in a plastic box dating all the way back to the late 1970s. And that sounds old, even to me.

Most anglers organize their fly box by fly type and hook size, color, and whether it's fished wet or dry. I organize my flies by the time period in which I tied them. For example, a box may only contain the old leftover ones from last year. Usually, the older fly boxes are full, so the most recent flies get a new fly box. As I was perusing through my vest, investigating various fly boxes and what I had stuffed in them, I proceeded to find a Sucrets box from 1978 bursting with flies of all sizes, shapes, and rusted hooks.

The old Sucrets boxes made great fly boxes. The hinges were rugged, and the aluminum boxes were light and would not rust. A person could change the flavors of Sucrets and the different flavor box colors would help distinguish between the various flies and their uses. I still carry a Sucrets box of old flies today.

Some years, I just rotate fly boxes. The old fly patterns popular decades ago tied by folks like Lee Wulf, Vincent Marinaro, and Art Flick still catch plenty of fish. Most of these patterns were tied with various types of animal hair, rooster and colored hen neck feathers. The internet has promoted newer versions of the older flies with synthetic materials and changed fly names to ones that resemble their family trees.

I went through a stage where a sleeve of every new synthetic material was purchased to pursue this passion. They caught fish and still do, and I found them somewhat easier to tie with. But in my old age, I again am beginning to revert to using natural materials such as fox fur, muskrat, angora, and snowshoe rabbit to tie with. Arthritic fingers are not quite as nimble and the older eyes not as sharp. Making the smaller sizes 20 to 24 is now nearly impossible. Even if I could tie them again, it would be difficult to attach these little guys to a leader.

There is always that one special fly that comes out perfect in your eyes. I may tie anywhere from 6-12 flies every time I sit down at the vise, depending on what is on television and how large a cocktail fixed, but there is that one special fly that turns out perfect. It looks so good that even I want to bite it.

It was a beautiful late spring day. I hiked the two miles along the Georgia side of the Chattooga River and crossed over it twice to get to this run above Reed Creek. The current is long, with just enough momentum to give a delicately laid fly a long, drag-free float. I noticed an unusually large rainbow that had perched his lips above the water's surface to inhale a delicious insect. Chill bumps and anticipation of a great tug are in order. I pulled out this one perfect fly that was manufactured while I watched Netflix the night before and got ready for battle.

Quietly, I wade into position, and there he is again. Rings form from his appearance. I have narrowed his feeding lane down to about five feet of river right below a small hemlock reaching out from an undercut bank. I decided on a long rollcast and let the fly drift right by the mossy rock and hemlock.

And then my picture-perfect cast was in the air. My tiny 6x tippet material wraps on one single hemlock limb hanging over the target area that I had previously paid no attention to. I am forced to make a decision: lose my perfectly tied fly or just go retrieve it and find some more fish rising and singing that same feeding hymn further up the river.

I hate fishing decisions. One should only have to stress over what to eat before going fishing and what time to leave the house. Coming home is not a decision. You leave when the fish quit biting.

Losing a perfect fly is almost like parting with a girlfriend, from what I have heard. If you lose one through no fault of your own (it may have gotten hung in the current on a rock, lost in a tree or laurel branch, or broke off on a fish), it softens the blow and makes it a little easier to rebound. You just get another one by reaching in the box, deciding what flavor fly to try, tying it on and keep fishing.

But you just fished with that perfect fly, which took extra time to tie and lost it from being hung up in a tree. A sense of frustration and sickness in the stomach appears. That fly took 25 minutes of meticulous preparation to be presentable to the fish. All the hackles that make it ride high in the water and float are perfect. The body is balanced with excellent proportions, and if you make one bad cast, it's over. The end with no takebacks.

Then you wade across the stream and put down every fish within 50 feet, cussing under your breath. You follow the fly line only to find that special fly hanging in a tree, wrapped once around a limb and dangling gingerly just out of reach. Do you climb the tree or just break it off?

At least you attempted to fetch it back but ruined a good trout run in the process and had to rebuild the entire leader before you tie on another fly. And you ask yourself, was all this worth it?

It is hard to lose a fly, throw away or even discard an old fly when cleaning out fly boxes to make room for freshly tied ones. The old ones stay lodged in like ancient pillars and are always there if needed. They will always represent a good time at the vise and on the water. I guess that makes me an old fly, too.

Take A Kid Fishing

"Take a kid fishing. You'll capture their imagination." ~ Max Hawthorne, <u>Kronos Rising</u>

Sharing the Wonders of Fly Fishing

Being a grandpa is one of life's greatest blessings, and sharing my passion of the outdoors and fly fishing with my grandson is humbling, rewarding and wonderful. He has been my shadow since he was old enough to crawl, and I was limber enough to get down there with him.

As a toddler, he would sit in my lap and together we tied flies, or as it is called in the toddler world, we made "fishies" out of fur and feathers. Hooks were cut off so each fishy could be stuffed in pants pockets and brought out at bath time. If they clogged the tub drain at my son-in-law's house it wasn't my problem.

To create the perfect fishy, an intense study of materials was performed. This included running fingers through rooster necks and saddle feathers because they were soft. The correct feather was selected based on its ability to tickle the tyer. There was always a complete and total fascination with the process. In the short attention span allotted, we managed to tie one fly completely.

At age four, he waded the river with me, and after several missed hookups, landed his first trout on a fly. I discovered that with every annual increase in age, there is a corresponding increase in attention span. But at this stage, after landing the first fish, it was time to throw rocks and make big splashes.

On one occasion, fishing with me at age five, we managed to land three fish before I lost him to stick boat racing and netting leaves. My attention span theory continued to prevail.

As he neared the adolescent age of six, he frequently asked to fish with Papa. Each answer was an emphatic 'yes,' so we often loaded up the car seat, grabbed some food, and were off. Goldfish, Cheetos, and M&M's were staples on each trip.

I remember one trip when the river was too high to wade safely, so we decided to go on a hiking and discovery mission instead. Eventually finding a nice log on the river's edge, we sat and talked, then raced stick boats, our second favorite river pastime. I never win.

Another prerequisite for being a grandpa is patience, and the desire to listen and not judge. On our adventures he talked incessantly, as he had a lot to say, and the world was so big. He began each topic with an enthusiastic tone and an inviting sense of adventure. I learned in depth about Spiderman, Transformers, the speed of Sonic, Megalodons, and what makes fish swim fast.

During other fishing trips, he discussed school, his friends, and getting home to visit his neighbor who had so much neat stuff. I heard about playing superheroes with mom and building forts inside on rainy days, sitting in the deer stand till dark, and then walking beside his dad holding the flashlight back to the truck. I doubt the light was ever held down on the ground to find the path, but it brightened two hearts at that moment. I heard about previous four-wheeler cruises around the North Georgia mountains, picnics with Mimi, playing in the mud at Grandpa's farm, and riding the tractor.

After several intense listening sessions streamside, it happened. He asked the question I had quietly prepared for in the back of my mind and was hoping would come later in his sub-adult years, around twelve. At that age, I could share my fly fishing philosophy with him and he would understand it.

"Papa," he said, looking stoic and serious, which insinuated I better buckle up for what's to come next, "Why do you like to fly fish so much?" There was a long pause coupled with a disorganized thought process as to how to answer a six-year-old with such a heavy question.

My plan for the day was to take him fishing and teach him how to really spit well without all the drool associated with it. But my immediate plans changed. Spitting could be taught later, I mused.

"Hmmm," I thought as we both sat quietly and stared at the river. I needed a moment of silence to organize my thoughts. I quickly realized my fly fishing philosophy would have to wait. The original speech included a discussion of how fly fishing and the rhythm of a river helps a person briefly escape reality for a mental rebirth. It would also encompass the importance of conservation efforts to keep our rivers clean and share with him the beautiful places trout live.

That sub-adult discussion would embrace thoughts about how challenging and immensely satisfying the sport is, a basic understanding of the river and entomology, what trout eat, when they feed, where to look for fish based on the currents, what flies to use, when to use them, and so much more. But it all would have to wait.

"Isn't the river pretty?" I said, pointing to the light reflecting on the water's surface. "Look at how the sun is bending its rays through the leaves and causing sparkles on the surface. It's like a thousand lightbulbs turned on at once and pointing down at the river from all angles.

"And it's really cool how all the different currents work separately to bring bugs and our flies down to the fish," I added, showing him the different foam lines meandering downstream. I reminded him of how the stick boats floated and bobbed along the same currents.

I asked, "How does it feel standing in the water and feeling the river push against your legs? This makes you feel a part of the river, doesn't it? Putting on waders and stepping into the current is like wearing your Sonic costume and becoming him! Being in the river makes you part of something really special."

He looked at me with a big grin and nodded yes. I was beginning to think I was indeed making progress.

"Listen, do you hear all the birds singing?" I asked. "So many melodies from different birds become an outdoor choir. And all you must do is stop and be quiet. Remember how much we enjoy overlooking the world at the precipice? As far as we both can see, mountain tops reaching skyward with their tips punching holes in the clouds."

"All of that's part of fly fishing too. Every time we go fly fishing, we get to see, feel, and hear all of this. Now isn't that pretty cool?"

With a mouthful of Goldfish and M&M's he sputtered a yes and reinforced it with a nod. And before the next handful of nutrition, he asked, "Can we go catch another fish now?"

There it was, my opportunity to circle the conversation back to fishing. As we both stood up and adjusted our wader straps, somewhat stiff from sitting so low down on the rock, I replied with a question, "What do you like most about fly fishing?"

"Papa, this is fun! I like how the flyrod bends when a fish pulls on it. They are strong like Ironman."

I looked down at his expression, which had never changed from a smile and replied, "Don't we always have fun when we go fishing?"

I have discovered that one very simple word captivates both young and old when talking about fly fishing. The word is 'fun.' And because it came from the mouth of a six-year-old, it must be true. Everybody needs some form of fun in their life and the smile that comes with it.

I bent down to get a hug and asked, "Ready for another adventure?"

I grabbed his hand as we started wading along the river's edge, and he looked up and asked, "Now, where did you say that big fish lived? Bring the net 'cause I'm going to need it!"

Take a Kid Fishing

"Take a kid fishing. You'll capture their imagination." ~ Max Hawthorne, <u>Kronos Risin</u>

At the beginning of the flyfishing class each semester at Clemson University, I ask the students individually about their fishing adventures and experiences. Within each class are different levels of skills and backgrounds. All students have the same common denominator: they want to catch a fish.

Sadly, there are always a few students who have never been fishing. During the brief time we are together, each semester provides a remedy for this ailment. They have never experienced the outdoors in a manner that requires a tug on a rod, the lake at sunset, the smell of the salt marsh, the popping noise of a receding tide in the soft mud, or the life of a river rushing through their legs while wading.

Are we too busy or caught up in life and making a living, fighting a pandemic, or what? I don't know the answer, but I try to share my fishing experiences with each student. It's an obligation to the sport that I don't take lightly.

I often think about the first fish my three-year-old grandson caught. We decided to use nightcrawlers, and he loved sticking his fingers in the bait can and feeling the wormy squiggles.

He was totally fascinated and would hold a nightcrawler in his hand loosely, giggle, and gingerly place it back into the bucket. Then, of course, he wipes his nose with the same hand. He was off to a good start growing from a toddler to a little boy. Teaching him to spit would be next on my list!

The little fellow was upset at first when I put a long, juicy nightcrawler on the hook. I assured him the hook was only temporary and these were magic fishing worms. When submerged, they could talk the fish into biting them. His facial expression had a moment of skepticism. Once underwater, I said, these magic worms would speak fish talk, and I promised we wouldn't have to wait long for a fish to bite.

I had bought him a small five-foot ultra-light spinning rod that almost bent down to the handle. He said goodbye and dropped the worm off the side of the dock, and within seconds, a fish was on! As I settled his level of excitement down to where he could listen, I reminded him always to believe his Papa when it came to fishing.

"Papa, Papa," he hollered as the little rod bent in half. "What do I do now?"

Together, we began to land the fish. I lightly held the rod with him while he gritted his teeth and reeled like there was no tomorrow. He exclaimed with bubbling enthusiasm that the magic worms really worked! An excellent two-pound catfish was landed, pictures were taken, the fish rubbed, the interesting whiskers on each side of his mouth pulled, and then he was released. What a wonderful memory and reward that will forever be with me.

Every student who desires to learn deserves a chance to catch a fish. From casting on ponds to wading rivers or easing along in the coastal marsh, once that experience happens, in most cases, it really becomes more than just catching fish.

Most states I have researched have programs that promote the "Take a Kid" philosophy, which is great. There are numerous other websites on Google I discovered promoting those programs.

During the last 21 (as of 2020) years, I have had students sit on the riverbank and cry after catching their first fish ever and on a fly rod. Emotions were overrun with tears and joy. I once accidentally stepped in neck-deep in a river trying to net a fish for a young lady who hooked her very first fish but couldn't coerce it towards the bank. Wet and smiling, together we landed the fish and took pictures. I learned a valuable lesson many years ago: always take extra clothes when wading a river. The stories could go on and on.

It's all the smiles and excitement from being alongside a "fish newbie" when they land that first fish and begin a contagious journey that I hope will last a lifetime. The importance of teaching young people about fishing the fragile environments where they live cannot be stressed enough.

My class has started pond fishing now as casting practice continues. Soon, we'll be in the river. There's a child in all of us every time a fish is caught. I am blessed to be part of this experience with so many great young people.

I received a text from a former student of mine from ten years ago. I could feel his excitement as I read the text. He stated, "Best lesson you taught me in class was to teach someone else to fish. I taught a friend how to fish today and he a caught fish!"

Teach or take someone fishing with you who has never been before. Make it fun for them first, and the rest will follow. The satisfaction and thrill you will experience are priceless.

First Fishing Trip with Dad

The old neighborhood is lined with houses. The woods we played in now hold an abundance of brick, mortar and siding. The little creek, which once had a consistent flow from the spillway of a pond hidden back in the woods near Augusta Road, is dry. Driving through the subdivision brings happy memories and melancholy recollections to see how it has changed. But then again, everything has changed. Even the creek.

The creek itself was an imaginative place, where sticks became boats and were raced around rocks. Small dams were built to increase the water level where small boys could sit and cool off in the hot summer weather. Jacuzzi was not a word in our vocabulary, but we understood the definition. Swimming trunks and bathing suits were reserved for pools. In the creek, short pants were acceptable and would eventually dry if we stayed outside long enough.

Aggravating crayfish with skinny sticks and seeing how long they could stay clamped on these bits of wood brought an intense competitiveness in a group of youngsters. One needed to pull them slowly, only inching the crayfish across the sandy bottom to intersect with the make-believe finish line.

I remember one day Dad came home and promised a fishing trip to Lake Hartwell the following weekend. He said we would rent a boat and motor from the marina and crappie fish. It didn't matter what kind of fish we were after, just the excitement about being with Dad and fishing together. Dad worked many long hours in the textile industry, so there wasn't always a lot of spare time.

I didn't have any concept as to how large Lake Hartwell was. I just knew that if there was a motor involved, it was bigger than our little half-acre piece of heaven hidden in the woods several hundred yards upstream.

The fishing anticipation in a young boy made bedtime a struggle. Burning thoughts of the fish, what kind, how big, being in a boat for the first time, danced fervently throughout my head and kept my eyes wide open. I had so many questions, and Dad repeatedly told me to be patient. What did the word patient mean?

I wondered how Dad knew where to go find fish, but it really didn't matter. This sense of excitement and ardent thoughts of an upcoming fishing adventure still make it hard for this boy, 60 years later, to sleep the night before. And I hope it never changes.

The day before our quest I can remember Dad coming home with a new bait bucket. He grabbed a pillowcase from the linen closet and took me down to the creek. He found a long
oak stick that had fallen near the creek bottom. I was instructed to find a large rock for the bottom of the pillowcase. I can recall him telling me that as a boy growing up in north Georgia, he used a burlap potato sack as it drained better and wished we had one.

We walked up to where the creek made a hard right around a boulder and formed a deep pocket on the inside near tree roots that had been washed out. At age six, a deep run was defined as about 18 inches. I could see small minnows in large numbers darting in and out of the tree roots.

He took the pillowcase and opened it up where the current would wash inside and laid the big rock on the bottom to hold it down. My job was to stand behind it and keep the pillowcase open. He took the stick and jabbed inside the tree roots. I could feel the pillowcase wiggle with life forms swimming. After a few minutes, he grabbed the pillowcase and lifted it up quickly, pouring all the inhabitants into the new minnow bucket, now filled with creek water. Like seeing new toys on Christmas morning for the first time, I stared at all the minnows, crayfish, and a turtle that we had caught with a keen sense of anticipation and excitement. Everything managed to get released except the minnows.

In a little boy's mind, this swirling school of delectable bait needed an extra layer of protection. So, that night I slept with the minnow bucket in my bedroom. Of course, Mom wasn't really fond of that idea, but Dad overruled. After all, the minnows were needed for the most important task at hand; bringing bigger fish back home!

That next morning, I was awake when Dad peeped in the room and called my name. I had already gotten up and dressed to save time. There was a difference between getting up for school and a fishing trip.

Miles to a fishing destination seems longer getting there than coming home. We arrived at the marina, and they had the rental boat and motor fueled and waiting for us. I loaded the rods and carefully placed the minnow bucket against the boat seat for more support. The little aluminum 14' V hull looked like a yacht in my eyes. My first fishing trip with Dad and my first boat ride. It was almost too much excitement for a small boy to handle. Excitement could also be defined as hyper, and I was told several times, in a fatherly voice, to slow down, hush, and sit on the front seat near the bow.

Of course, I kept opening the top of the minnow bucket to make sure they hadn't jumped out. I also liked to stick my hand in the bucket and feel them tickle as they swam through my fingers. For some genetic reason, my daughter always enjoyed the same sort of tickle.

I could never remember our location or how many crappie we caught. I do remember that I learned how to hook a minnow, how the red and white bobber connected to the line and how intently I concentrated on it. I remember having lunch in the boat and just being alone with Dad fishing. Photographs weren't taken but the pictures will linger in my mind forever.

He didn't know it then, but he created a love for fishing that has lasted a lifetime. One never knows how impactful and positive a day fishing with a youngster can be. Maybe that's why I always like to "take a kid" fishing.

Cocoa for Christmas

Mattie had been our family pet and Dad's hunting companion for four years. She had developed into a loving, affectionate family member and, in our eyes, a true field champion. I can remember Dad bragging about her retrieving skills to anyone who would listen.

Being only eight then, I don't remember much of her younger years, much less mine. I can vividly remember the long black nose rising above the table's edge, looking for a handout, spills or crumbs. Those sad-looking eyes of neglect, tirelessly and quietly begging, usually won out with Mom and me. And when guests were having dinner with us, Mattie pitifully laid her head in their laps to show neglect. But we knew differently. She had perfected this act, and the kitchen table was her stage.

During dove season, I can vividly remember when Mattie would go sit by the door while Dad was gathering his gun and shells. He would jab a comment to his buddies, noting she was also thinking about hunting birds and waiting for him to hurry.

This year, hunting season would be different as Mattie wouldn't accompany Dad much. It seems her season had come in unexpectedly near the middle or end of the September dove season. Mother Nature took charge, and she "accidentally" mated up with Mr. Davis's chocolate lab. Dad found them on the edge of the soybean field, but it was too late.

At first, Dad was mad at Mattie for getting pregnant. I believed it was more out of selfishness, knowing he would not have his canine buddy beside him when he raised his gun to fire and would be forced to retrieve his own birds or send me for them. She was so much faster than me and didn't complain. In an exasperated tone, he would comment she was more obedient too.

But on the other hand, the family was excited about the puppies. Mom began making a whelping box and getting all the supplies ready. It didn't take Mattie long to start showing, and she became more lethargic, lying around the house as the puppies grew inside her. After school, she and I would hike along the dirt road behind the house over to the pond for exercise. As we walked, I threw sticks and kicked rocks, all the while talking to her about how much I hated school. Her tail was constantly wagging as I spoke. I thought she understood. Sometimes, she would wander off to sniff fallen dead limbs and brush piles, flushing songbirds for fun.

It wasn't long until I started begging Mom and Dad for a puppy, explaining in great detail and repeating nightly how responsible I was becoming. This topic became the object of most dinner conversations. Dad finally gave me a detailed list of chores most eight-year-olds should be doing daily, and I did my best to keep up with them. Occasionally, a meltdown would occur and I would sneak off with Mattie to the pond. One evening, a pair of wood ducks twirled and twisted along the pond's edge. She stopped, sat, watched, and whimpered as they acrobatically went out of sight. She was getting restless, and we all knew it would happen soon.

One morning, somewhere around two weeks before Thanksgiving, Dad woke me before daylight and we walked out to the whelping box. There lay Mattie, exhausted with eight chocolate and black fur balls. Whimpering with their eyes closed, Mattie nudged them close. I immediately noticed a tiny, short-nosed chocolate puppy, smaller than the rest. I gently picked her up and snuggled her in my sweatshirt.

I stayed home from school that day. Dad said that the births of additional family members made a good excuse to play hooky. We checked on the puppies and Mattie every little while, and I would always turn the cute puppy begging into a groveling show.

I regularly crawled in the whelping box, rubbed Mattie behind the ears, and cuddled all of her young. I had never experienced "puppy breath" and found it magical. The smell was fresh and clean; I thought it resembled a sweet milk aroma. I frequently placed all eight puppies on my stomach and neck, listening to their muted whimpers while crawling and pricking me with their tiny claws. But it was the "puppy breath," the amazing, fragrant smell of newborn, cuddly furballs that seemed to make me snuggle each one close.

The little short-nose chocolate won my heart. I would lay her on my face, and she would sniff my forehead and nuzzle my ear and neck, then tuck herself in the folds of my arm and sleep. I dared not move and wake her; I just lay there motionless and smiled. Puppies have a way of making you feel warm inside when holding them.

This became a daily ritual before and after school and again after my new daily chores. As they began to grow, so did my desire for a puppy. I wrote Mom and Dad a note listing reasons to keep a puppy. I described how a puppy would give me a special companion I could responsibly learn to help care for. She would be home waiting for me every day, could sleep with me, and become my best friend. And besides, I explained to Dad how I wanted to be an expert dog trainer like him, and he could teach me with my puppy. Not to mention, Mattie would also need a playmate.

After about three weeks, their eyes began to open as they became stronger. Their big round eyes could look into your soul and launch a soft bond of tenderness and compassion. Their soft fur made them totally irresistible and hard to put down. Once down, it was time for a belly rub and playtime.

During this time, my grades even picked up. The little chocolate female was special. She was the runt of the litter. Being somewhat smaller than the rest, I would always place her in a prime position to feed. As she grew, I watched her clumsily follow me around the yard, exploring all things new. I imagined her eventually growing into her feet and hoped the tail never quit wagging the dog.

Watching the puppies grow became a social event. Several nights a week, Dad's hunting buddies would come and check on the puppies' status, pick up a few to hold, and talk about the birds they'd yet to retrieve. I figured Dad was looking for homes for the little ones. I always made sure everyone knew the little chocolate female was my favorite.

As Christmas crept closer, the pups slowly went out to new homes. Mom said Dad was really particular about who took the puppies and that Mattie would see her puppies on the dove fields in years to come.

They never committed to me keeping a puppy, but I kept hoping and begging. I had named the little runt Cocoa. Her coat was the color of hot chocolate with two melted marshmallows, so the name fit well.

There were two puppies left on Christmas Eve, Cocoa and another black female. At eight years old, the patience portion of my personality hadn't fully developed, and I knew it wore thin on my parents. Mattie seemed relieved she didn't have to take care of so many puppies anymore and started to regain some of her livelier and more playful instincts.

Before Christmas Eve dinner, the doorbell rang and one of Dad's buddies appeared ready to pick up his family's Christmas puppy. Crushed, I sat there quietly and almost in tears not knowing which pup was his. A huge sigh of relief overcame me as I realized he was taking the little black one. Only one puppy left. I spoke very little during dinner and then went out to tell Cocoa and Mattie good night. I sat out there holding Cocoa and rubbing Mattie, praying to the Christmas star for a miracle. "Please let me keep Cocoa," I repeated.

Mom and Dad appeared around the corner and told me it was time for bed as Santa Claus would be coming soon. I can't remember exactly, but I don't think I was asleep very long when Dad woke me and asked me to come into the den. The overhead lights were turned off with only the colored Christmas tree lights twinkling and the fireplace flickering a warm aura. Mattie had her backside to the hearth and lay sound asleep, content and warm.

I noticed a basket underneath the tree with a squirming blanket and a bow. I reached down to pick up the basket and recognized a familiar, distinguishing whimper I had come to love. I peeped in and there was my Cocoa with a red ribbon collar. I smiled, hugged Mom and Dad, and sat beside Mattie in front of the fireplace, holding my Cocoa. Mom leaned over and handed me a mug of my hot chocolate with two marshmallows. I had indeed gotten my Cocoa for Christmas after all.

A Cricket for A Bream

The hot, hazy time of summer was upon us. The school would be closed for three short months as words like "family vacation", "the lake", "the beach", and "swimming pool" would be spoken with incessant regularity in many kids' sentences. Kindergarten was now a memory, and the excitement of being a first grader hadn't set in yet for my daughter.

During this time of year, the interstate was buzzing with increased traffic flow. There were trucks loaded down with suitcases and coolers, golf carts in tow, and SUVs with car top carriers filled to the max, which was evidence summer had begun. But it was also another time. Summer days gave us more time to fish without having to worry about getting home early for homework and studies!

It was time to pull off the interstate and leave the congestion. The traffic noise would soon become silent as I backed my old Jon boat down a dirt road leading to the pond. She and I were having a father-daughter outing.

She had grown up around guns, fly rods, fishing stories, and boys and men wearing camouflage. Her interest in the outdoors was natural, and I had decided not to push her but instead would know when the time became right for her to tag along and participate.

When she was younger, we spent a lot of time together walking in the woods, sitting in a deer stand, and watching creatures. Making plaster casts of animal tracks and then bringing them home to identify them became a game to her. In her own way, she began an early appreciation of nature and all the wonderous-encompassing beauty.

It wasn't until she was grown that I realized the exposure to the woods, mountains, and streams had such a profound and wonderful impact. Spending time outdoors with her as a child will indeed provide memories that last a lifetime.

This day was an extra special one as *she* wanted to go fishing. Any previous plans of mine were immediately canceled, and I felt humbled to entertain this Cinderella. She wanted to fish in the pond across from the house, and it was decided that we would rise early and take "Rambo," her name for the Ford Bronco that I used to fish and hunt with, and drive around the pond and to create our own little dirt boat landing off the dams' spillway. I had taken the motor off the Jon boat to make it lighter and easier to load and unload. Keeping only the trolling motor would be sufficient.

The pond was about 15 acres and fairly deep, especially at the dam where we put it. The edges were enveloped with heavy grass along with several brush piles breaking the surface, good bream habitat. The full moon in May had been the week before, and I hoped the bream would still be bedding somewhat.

She insisted on having a picnic in the boat. Drinks, peanut butter and jelly sandwiches, and a few snacks were in order. The summer temps reached the mid-80s by late morning, and the crème-filled cookies were extremely runny, so we munched on them by holding the plastic packaging, which made the gooey middle run all over our face and hands. Washing off with cool pond water felt good, with the soaring temps and, of course, a little splashing on each other.

She had never been to the pond to fish but had paraded around the edge several times weekly with me to work our chocolate lab, Cocoa, on obedience and fetching. We usually came home a muddy mess. She noticed some rings in the water where rising bream had surface fed, and we talked about such important things.

As we left our makeshift portage area and eased across the pond, not one to be quiet for longer than three seconds, she began a barrage of questions–
What do fish eat?
How do they breathe underwater?
Who taught them swimming lessons?
Why are bass bigger than bream?
Do fish eggs float?
Will they eat my cookie if I put it on a hook?
Will the mother miss her baby if we keep a little one?
Are little bream making the little rings on top?

As I eased the anchor down near a small clump of water lilies, the perennial question was asked, "Daddy, why do people fish?"

We discussed the fish fry at Grandma's house and where the main food source came from, but we spent more time talking about being with family and friends with no interruptions, just like we were that day. I told her about trying to match wits with a creature that had a brain the size of a green pea but could consistently outsmart a person. We talked about the serenity and quietness of the water, and I pointed out the heron stalking fish along the water's edge. How habit-forming it was to feel the rod when a fish was hooked and feel its surging, tugging and diving theatrics.

Her brown eyes twinkled with intense curiosity.

The summer sun beat down with an intenseness that made the pond look more inviting for swimming than fishing, but we persevered. I didn't want the morning to end.

She was a touch timid at first about putting her hand in the cricket box, but courage and coaxing soon healed this issue. (On her next fishing trip she arranged all the worms neatly across the boat's bottom trying to pick the one that wiggled the most. Not to include the minnow bucket where she would giggle as they swam around the bucket and tickled her fingers.) Needless to say, I discovered crickets in the boat for weeks afterward.

It's hard for a seven-year-old to sit quietly in a classroom, much less be cramped in a 14' boat. While we waited on the corks to disappear below the water's surface, she began to investigate all my tackle boxes. I sat there quietly as she probed and rambled intently through the assortment of plugs, hooks, sinkers, and other miscellaneous tackle. I smiled every time she would look up and ask," What's this for?" a million times.

We kept switching out new and lively crickets for the drowned ones, trying to create some fish activity. Hearing several fish splash near her red and white bobber, her attention turned to fishing. Within a few short minutes, she hollered, "Look Daddy!" as the cork disappeared. I told her to grab the rod and gently lift the tip high in the air. For once she listened and followed directions without them being repeated. After setting the hook, a nice bream, followed by an erratic cork behavior, *broke the stillness.*

Determined not to actively get involved in playing the fish, I tried to merely help coach and encourage. She grunted and bent over, trying to crank the reel handle as fast as she could at first, but the ultralight rod brought her back to reality and forced her to slow down.

In what probably seemed like hours to her, but really just only a minute or two, she brought a nice bream boatside and proceeded to lay it firmly in my lap, hook and all. Her smile told the story as she sat back down and bragged about breaking her very own world record.

A "squeeze my guts out hug" and a "thank you Daddy for a fun morning" highlighted the beginnings of a lifetime of fishing adventures. Eventually, she traded the ultralight spinning rod for a fly rod and the live crickets for a foam imitation, but the crème filled cookie never changed.

Rivers and the Great Trout

"Granddad always said the best things about fishing were beyond the senses. He said the mountains, rivers and fish were the center of why you were there, but not the heart, that the heart was in those pure moments in and around the fishing, ……….. That's what hooked your soul."
— J.C. Bonnell, <u>*Burnt Tree Fork*</u>

The name Papa, sometimes called Grandpa or Grandad, comes with a rather large obligation. This responsibility includes spoiling the child, sharing great stories of which only tiny parts may be true, being able to communicate family history, and explaining the way life used to be when you were a boy. At the same time, this obligation allows Papa the opportunity to look at nature and its intrinsic gifts once again through the eyes of a child.

I embraced this job description and began fulfilling it several years ago. I started by taking my grandson, Rivers, fishing, always making it less about the fish and more about our time together. And while I am never too old to go drown worms with my grandson in a farm pond, I always have a fly rod within arm's reach.

The rivers and streams throughout the Southern Appalachian Mountains had been extremely low this year due to drought conditions. But fall was in the air, and cooler night temperatures meant cooler water and more active and feeding trout. Low water also meant easier wading for my 5-year-old grandson, so off we went. Low water conditions may prove to be an asset when your "little buddy" is only 41 inches tall.

The fishing expectations of my little buddy seemed to multiply the closer we got to the river. This included asking all the questions that could cross the mind of a five-year-old that, while simple to me, were of the utmost importance to him.

He had been fishing with me many times before, but each new occasion was like the first time he's ever been. The many questions revealed the excitable anticipation bottled up inside him, which reminded me of myself. I never get tired of wading mountain streams and hope I never do. I was glad to have my little buddy sharing the river with me.
.
Football and hunting season always reduce the number of fall fly fishermen on the river, which is alright with me. Today we would have the river to ourselves, accompanied by a close friend to help watch out for my little grandson.

Together, Rivers and I had tied flies for our outing the night before. After completing each fly, he asked that I cut the hooks off so he wouldn't hurt himself when grabbing them from his pocket. I explained the hook part was what held the fish on the fly, and he could keep these flies to show his friends in kindergarten. We would fish with my flies and be extra careful. He understood, I think.

The creative imagination a child has is astounding. We began discussing why one needs waders instead of just getting wet, even though they may be a bit uncomfortable. The water is cold, which he soon discovered. He compared the protection of waders to the cloaks and suits of his superheroes – "Iron Man" had protection from bad guys thanks to his "waders of armor."

"Even the Ghost Busters team wear white, protective clothing to protect them from the 'slimers and goo," I said, continuing to relate to his hero friends.

"I understand, Papa, we need protection to fish here," he acknowledged, while in the same breath, he added, "And can we watch the new Ghost Busters movie again tonight, right?"

I knew where we could enter the river in a very shallow stretch and explained there was a rope lying down on the bank with knots to help us hang on. We could pick it up and use it as a handrail while walking backward down the steep bank. This seemed exciting until he saw it, looked down the riverbank, and then climbed on my shoulders as I backed my way to the river.

After ankle-deep water covered both our sets of wading shoes, he talked to me about how dry he was and how cool the waders really were. The protection was working. Then he stuck his arm down into the water about shoulder length and picked up a rock and threw it. So much for having a dry day!

He never complained about being wet. Eventually, both arms were scooping up rocks when not fishing, and the two of us practiced throwing like baseball pitchers.

I had to be careful when wading with him in clear water. He felt confident if he could see the bottom, and confidence usually breeds overconfidence and a river bath. After a couple nice "pullbacks" on his wader straps, he automatically started walking right beside me as we maneuvered through the translucent river.

We discussed the importance of wading quietly as we watched a heron moving gently but deliberately along the riverbank in front of us. We talked about the stalking heron and how we need to be like him as we move, looking for good runs and pocket water to fish.

I whispered and told him that fish could hear us, so we needed to walk without splashing. He knew fish didn't have ears, so a simplified discussion took place about how fish hear through vibrations.

He saw my wading staff and decided he needed one as well. We began a search to find the perfect beaver stick his size. As adults, we take for granted the value of a walking staff or cane, but this little guy didn't understand. Once I explained how to put the stick down and use it for balance, both in the river and up the mountain, he and his stick became inseparable. He used it all day, never lost it, and brought it home to be used on the next adventure.

A touch of independence surfaced at first as he struggled to roll cast like we had practiced at home. So, I offered to cast for him, not to mention it would keep the amount of tangled tippet to a minimum. I explained how the river splits around rocks and the current causes foam lines, which is where we would cast and look for trout.

 I had tied on a lightly weighted woolly bugger in size 16. On the second drift through the run, the trout hit the fly, and I lifted up the rod and handed it to him. Today, after three lost fish and a little coaxing, he finally realized he needed to be gentler and keep the fly rod tip up.

His competitive nature perked up, and from the fourth fish on, he played each one into the net by himself, listening intently to my coaching as the fish dashed and splashed and tried to pull the rod tip down, and him with it.

The trip was not only about catching fish. I held his hand while he balanced himself walking across logs and fallen timber. We practiced our rock-throwing skills and made big splashes when not fishing. But it was the stick boat racing that he seemed to love most. We learned how the river's currents and eddies flowed by watching our stick boats of different sizes float along the fast and slow currents.

We kicked leaves along the mountain trail, stumbled over small stickup roots, and approached our last fishing spot as the sun began to dip behind mountains. As we neared the last set of small rapids, the river made a hard left and then straightened up and filtered over a small dam of stones.

Climbing down the bank was easy, and we positioned ourselves along the river edge where I could cast back into the foam line. After several casts, my grandson told me it was time to change flies because this one may be tired, and we needed a fresh one. I made one more cast with the "tired" fly and a hook-up! I handed him the rod, not knowing what I had hooked, only that the rod tip bent almost halfway down to the handle.

He stood stoically with laser focus as this fished peeled line off the single action fly reel. His hands were placed perfectly on the cork, gripping so intently that I could see his neck muscles tighten up. Such determination. The previous fish were just practice compared to this one.

I never touched the rod to assist, but chose instead to coach from beside him. And he listened. The fish dove into the pool above and attempted to entrench itself underneath the bank, but his subtle rod pressure was enough to divert the fish.

Instead, it broke water and thrashed from one side of the river to the other, trying to dislodge the small fly. The trout never followed the current downstream, which could have been a disaster. Finally, after six minutes of battle, the combat was almost over. The trout rode the gentle side of the current and was netted quickly.

Pictures were taken, but the excitement of a five-year-old landing a fish over half his size by himself on a fly rod for that duration and never wavering is a memory we both will never forget. The smiles, fist pumps, high fives, and water stomping are priceless. He was proud and I was proud of him. Papa was a spectator during the battle of this great, beautiful brown trout. This time, it was truly all about the fish!

Acknowledgments

Thank you Addi Michele Frazier for your illustrations and creativity.

A Special "Thank You" goes out to Joey Frasier, editor of *South Carolina Wildlife* magazine for continuing to inspire stories for the magazine and this book.
Several of the stories were also published in *South Carolina Wildlife* magazine, including:
A Winter Fishing Dream
Cocoa for Christmas
Boys Ponds, and Big Creatures
Rivers and the Great Trout

No book is complete and polished without the benefits and evil eye of a great editor. Thank you, Kathleen Brady and Joey Frazier, for the time you spent pouring over this manuscript and adjusting my commas and apostrophes. It's greatly appreciated.

 A special thanks to my long-time family friend and fishing buddy, Dave Armstrong.
His photo editing and expertise has proven invaluable in helping design the cover photo.

Kurt Kenison, a great friend, is not forgotten for fishing with Rivers and I and taking those wonderful pictures of Papa and Rivers together.

A special thanks to Laura Wiggins, the artist of my favorite Labrador and hunting companion, Kasper, as shown in the chapter of Dreams and Desires. This drawing has been cherished for more than 25 years

Jim Mize, a friend who also mentored me with his writing and publishing skills. His books include; The Winter of our Discount Tent, A Creek Trickles Though It, Hunting with Beanpole, Fishing with Beanpole, and his most recent book, The Jon Boat Years.

And the team at riversandfeathers.com, including WebspeakMedia.com

About the Author

Mike Watts is a Freelance writer and Publisher of riversandfeathers.com, a website devoted to short stories about fly fishing. He has chased fish on the fly in the Southern Appalachians for over 47 years.

During this time, he served in many capacities in the local TU Chapter, is a Life Member in Trout Unlimited, and served on the SC Department of Natural Resources Freshwater Advisory Board, along with several other organizations promoting the sport. He feels its important to also give back to the sport by volunteering to organizations such as: Casting Carolina, Casting for Recovery, and several Boy Scout and Girl Scout troops.

Mike enjoys teaching and sharing his wisdom, tall tales, advice, stories and maybe a few lies about the fish he caught somewhere.

Since 2004, this fly fishing fanatic has taught fly fishing part-time at Clemson University under the auspices of the Parks Recreation & Tourism Department/Leisure Skills. Students receive one hour of credit for course completion. He was instrumental in establishing a Fly Fishing Club at Clemson which is considered one of the largest student fly fishing clubs nationally.

Publisher

We are your ultimate destination for all author's services. Book writing, marketing, publishing and editing- we offer it all under one roof. Our dedicated team of industry experts is here to support and guide you on your authorial journey. From crafting compelling stories to editing, proofreading, and formatting, we ensure your manuscript shines. Embrace your literary aspirations with us and unlock your full potential as an author

bookpublishingpulse.com